Drawn to the Enemy

Barbara Winkes

ISBN: 978-1-7781247-5-4

Created with Atticus

For D.

Prologue

Two years ago

The man kept his hand on his weapon, aware that it was trembling slightly. Failure was not an option. In fact, it would be fatal. He cursed his charge for running off without waiting for him, into what could be an ambush. His opponents—business partners, as he called them—were not to be trusted, but then again, the same could be said about the man's employers. Blackmailers. Same difference. He stepped out of the light of the streetlamp and into the shadows of the dark alley.

He could hear voices getting more agitated.

What a fool, expecting him to clean up his messes time after time. And the man would, because he, too, had made his choices. For him and his wife to enjoy a comfortable life, their kids receiving an excellent education at their private schools.

Everything had a price.

Everyone had a price.

He couldn't afford to be distracted. That could be fatal too.

He carefully inched closer to where he could see the outline of the two men, raised voices telling him that their argument was about to turn physical. Once again, he was asking himself how the hell he had gotten to his point. He used to have…principles? He almost laughed out loud. Too little too late.

When he saw the glint of a knife, he pulled the trigger.

One of the men dropped to the ground, the other one looked around frantically before he ran.

The man assumed that the prince would wait for him at the car. Silly boy.

He went over to the fallen adversary to make sure he wouldn't bother them again tonight, the color draining from his face when he got a good look at him.

"Oh no," he muttered, lightheaded with the sight and what it meant. "Fuck, no. No, no."

In his mind, he went through a multitude of worst-case scenarios. Most of them had him end up dead as well. Then he saw the plastic card on the ground. A credit card, left behind by the runner.

He picked it up and pocketed it, taking a last look around to make sure no one had witnessed the incident.

The few windows that belonged to residents had stayed dark. Whoever had the bad fortune to live here, knew better than to talk to the police.

Unbelievable. He was safe.

He hurried back to the car and took off, resisting the urge to blast the radio at its highest volume.

Safe, if he played his cards right.

He was going to miss the fool. Prince. *Sorry*, he thought. *Better you than me.*

Chapter One

Courtney

I desperately need a break. That's not the same as running away, is it? It might be in the cards sometime soon, if there's no alternative, but it's not my intention now. A couple of weeks in the city, away from the weight of obligations and revelations should do the trick.

I need to clear my mind, figure out what is fact, and what is imagination. About Tommy's death, and the future Oliver and I are going to have.

We left this morning, early enough to avoid an awkward conversation at the breakfast table. I bought us sandwiches at the train station, a venti coffee for me, and a hot chocolate for Oliver. He thinks it's all a big adventure, and I want to keep up the illusion as long as possible.

Illusions, I have few of them left. If they haven't already, I'm certain that Rory and Ciara could track me easily, find out what train we're on, what hotel we will check into.

I tried to be stealthy, be my usual polite self, not raise any controversy, though it's been a lot harder lately.

3

We have all been coming out of the worst of grief, but we're dealing with this new reality differently. Or perhaps not so differently, projecting our hopes and dreams onto my four-year-old son who is blissfully ignorant of all of it as he's engrossed in his princess coloring book.

I suppress a smile remembering one dinner last week when Rory just barely stopped himself from making a comment. It took only one look from Ciara, a raised eyebrow, to make him rein in that comment. Their hearts are in the right place, I think. Most of the time.

Earlier, a teenaged person with pink streaks in their blonde hair sat across from us for a few stops, and they gave Olli a thumbs up, to his delight.

As a parent, it's easy to get drawn into assumptions, when you should love them above all. That's always the priority for me. I want to believe it was that for Rory and Ciara as well, though they raised Tommy differently. Family and loyalty matter. Maybe even love. But they also need an heir, a man of the house. This is where our differences come in.

Tommy made a choice, with all the possible consequences that came with it. The price was too high, for him, for all of us. I have to draw my own conclusions, and this is why I dragged my son out of bed at an ungodly hour to leave the mansion and get out of town.

I've been breathing easier with every stop, every mile farther away from home, which tells me nothing I didn't already know.

This time will be good for us. It will determine the future, and no matter what anyone thinks, it's up to me to make those decisions. I'd like to think Tommy would see it the same way. I doubt it. But he's not here, and I have a child to protect above all else.

Finally, the train rumbles into the station. After we check into the hotel, it will be time for lunch and a nap, likely for both of us. I already lined up our luggage, but when I ask Oliver for the coloring book and pencils, he protests.

"Mommy! I'm almost done!"

"You can finish at the hotel," I promise him, aware that there's a line forming behind me. Our fellow travelers' gazes range from bored to annoyed. I see the teenager from before giving me a smile.

"But I want to..."

"Sweetie, we're here now. We're going to get you some chicken nuggets, and later we'll go see Jade, remember?"

His eyes light up, his enthusiasm reminding me of someone else I knew, all those years ago before he became a stranger. It makes me even more determined.

"I like Jade," Oliver says, and, to my relief, lets me pack away the pencils and book. If I were a character in a romance novel, I might be letting out a breath I didn't know I was holding. I know I was holding it because I'm close to being lightheaded.

No time for that. I grab the handle of my suitcase, put his little backpack over my shoulder along with my purse, take his hand, and off we go.

I can hear a few mumbles behind us, but we make it to the platform and out of the train station without incident. We get into a cab and only fifteen minutes later, arrive at the Hotel Grand Palace. I used up a lot of points and all the online offers I was able to combine, knowing this might be one of the last times I'm able to offer us such frivolous luxury.

Funny, that I'm thinking in these terms already, only hours after I've left. Life with the Flynns was all that and then some, but it might come to an end sooner than later.

We had some snacks on the train earlier. Oliver never says no to one, and I had to calm my nerves, irrationally fearing that someone might come after us. It's a good thing we ate. There's a small line at reception.

Out of habit, clutching Oliver's hand, I take a look around, familiarize myself with my surroundings. Exits. Sometimes I don't know if I picked it up before, even when I had no clue what was going on, or if sudden loss created it. An experience like that certainly reinforces caution. Or paranoia.

My gaze lands on a tall blonde woman with perfectly coiffed hair standing by herself at a high table. She was probably lucky and checked in before the rush. Not that there is a rush now.

In a complete contrast to my earlier frantic preoccupation, I notice the way the dark blue dress hugs every one of her curves. She's wearing high heels, a blazer over her arm, her purse sitting on the table next to her. She's all class and elegance, and has me flustered for no reason, especially when she catches me ogling her, and the corners of her lips turn upwards into an amused smile.

"Good morning!"

The cheery smile of the hotel employee doesn't give anything away, though I can tell from her tone and slightly raised voice that it's not the first time she's addressing me. Feeling my face redden, I finally give her my full attention.

"Courtney Flynn," I say, blushing even harder, as if the employee cared at all. Saying my name, my married name, jolts me out of any stray fantasy about the stunning woman standing a few feet away. "I reserved a room online."

I thought I was unsettled before. It seems to take forever until she hands me my keycard, and Oliver and I can finally go up to our room.

When we pass by the woman, she's on the phone, but still for some inexplicable reason, holding my gaze.

I nearly run into another hotel guest who has just arrived, and that probably serves me right.

What the hell am I doing?

———eee———

I'm still not hungry, but we walk the few steps to a fast-food restaurant nearby to get Oliver his favorite for lunch. We've only just arrived. Between hanging out with Jade, and following my plans for the next few days, there will be healthier options.

As predicted, he's out for the count moments after we are back at the hotel, and after tucking him in, I use the time for a long hot shower. Given my earlier, puzzling reaction, a cold one might have been in order, but I need all the comfort I can get.

Even with the warmer spring day, I've been cold since this morning, which might have to do with little to no sleep last night, and others before, and too many nerves.

Time to ease up a little. I don't have to look over my shoulder here, at least not for the next few days. No one knows.

And if I stared at that woman a little too long, who can blame me? She was exquisite, I remember as the hot water rains down on me, and completely out of my league. Abruptly, I turn off the water and wrap myself in one of the huge fluffy towels, feeling awkward being naked, even if it's just me and my muddled thoughts. I once believed Tommy was out of my league too, and see what happened.

My baggage aside, I'm clearly the complete opposite of her. I could never get my hair to cooperate like that, even with pricey hairdressers. I can be clumsy, my near collision with the other guest case in point, though I guess I could sell that as part of my charm.

What is wrong with me? I'll never see her again. She probably thought I was ridiculous. And I have bigger problems to address.

Yet, her image lingers on my mind, which is intriguing and strange. No one has had this effect on me—since Tommy.

Chapter Two

Sienna

I'm here for business, which means my attention is single-mindedly focused, or at least it has been for most of the morning. Meetings, contracts with investors, discussing events and marketing campaigns for the chain, it's keeping me busy.

Or it should, but my thoughts keep wandering back to the woman I saw in the lobby. I must admit that every once in a while, a guest like her catches my eye, younger, adorable, carefree, the whole package, a blessed contrast to my own life. Not that I'm ungrateful. While I worked hard to get into my position, I'm not naïve enough to ignore that I had a leg up, and that people will remember. That means I have to work even harder to prove to everyone, including myself, that I belong here, that the people who put their trust in me didn't do so for sentimental reasons, but because they knew I could handle myself in a high-pressure environment.

It doesn't leave a lot of room for romance, but I'm not complaining. Occasionally, one of those younger, adorable women finds herself in my company, in the private suite I keep for multiple reasons. Mostly, to work in peace, but sometimes, to discreetly fulfill the needs of a woman who doesn't have time to date.

I am back in my suite after the last meeting, wondering about her. That's likely all I'll do in this case, because when she passed me by earlier, I saw something in her doe eyes that made me back off. Pain. That, combined with the boy holding on to her hand, is a red flag. At first, I thought she might be the nanny, but when no other adult showed up, and I saw them up close for a moment, I realized he was hers.

A child isn't necessarily a problem either, but there was something about her that spelled trouble. And it's the last thing I need right now when things have been going so well on our side. The Moretti family has all but disappeared from the picture. The few of them that are not locked up for attempted murder are keeping a low profile, aware of new and improved alliances.

Speaking of alliances. And attempted murder.

With the sweeping new developments we are taking on for new hotel projects, including a couple of huge resorts, the ridiculous rumors and accusations that have followed us should be a thing of the past.

Tomorrow, I'll have an interview with a prestigious fashion magazine—seems counterintuitive, but it will go a long way to link our business to its original prestige. It's a big moment for us, and I intend to enjoy every second of it, after years of damage control.

On the weekend, I'll have a little celebration with Aunt Simona and Uncle Francesco.

I am quite proud of my achievements, my ability to turn the ship around in what was one hell of a shitstorm, pardon my mixed metaphors. Their pride in me means a lot.

I don't care for distractions, but this one was...interesting. I might push my luck and find out what room she's in, and how long she's staying. No time like the present.

⸺ele⸺

The contracts were vetted by our lawyers a long time ago, so all I have to do is file them away. I go over the questions for the interview again and find I'm well prepared. I always am.

I send a text to Aunt Simona, *It's done*, and wait for her immediate response.

Congratulations! We can't wait to see you on Saturday.

I put my phone aside and step to the window, look outside at the city at my feet. The sun is starting to set, a dramatic spectacle from my point of view. I can't help smiling.

They couldn't keep us down for long, but they had no idea how strong we would come back. You don't mess with a Caruso. Keeping the peace, seeking revenge for those outrageous accusations—it will be in our hands.

I look forward to seeing Simona and Francesco, but I do feel like a little private celebration myself.

Just out of curiosity, I check reservations.

I'm not often taken off guard, but I have to admit, I am, just a little, when I see the name. I check all the information, and it all fits. Then I search her online, and shake my head, at myself, at her.

Courtney Flynn.

Courtney fucking Flynn. She's adorable all right, the Flynns' widowed daughter-in-law, and now other things make a lot more sense too. It's not up to me or certain needs of mine anymore. I have to keep an eye on her. Even though those contracts are signed, her presence here, at this time, can't be a coincidence. Was she mocking me?

I decide that was likely not the reason. In the Flynn family, she basically disappeared behind the imposing figures, her husband and her in-laws, quietly taking care of her son. I never met her before, obviously, but I heard that she keeps an ultra-low profile, not involved with the business.

That look she gave me though was interesting. Telling. Deer-in-the-headlights when she realized I caught her checking me out.

I decide to find her and figure out what she knows. At this point, complications are unacceptable.

Chapter Three

Courtney

Home sweet home, at least for the next couple of weeks. After that...I probably can't avoid any awkward conversations, even if my plan works out. There are still a few faults in its design. I can't deny that my in-laws did a lot for Oliver and me after what happened to Tommy. Okay, so they insisted on a prenup, but given that I was young and naïve at some point, and signed it, they could have kicked us out.

Part of me still wonders, would they have kicked *me* out, if it hadn't been for Oliver? Family matters, but I was the outsider, the one that was out of the loop.

Naïve, yes, I guess I have to own up to that, but how was I supposed to know how much money a business makes importing whiskey and other spirits? All I knew was that they had money, and I didn't ask too many questions as to where it came from. That seemed...Inappropriate? Impolite? Tommy never made much of an effort to share, and then he was gone, and I was a single mother with a toddler. The value of whiskey wasn't high on my priority list before. I couldn't afford to immerse myself in grief, and so Oliver became the sole focus.

He still is, but I've been more awake lately, slowly understanding what I've been missing.

Rory has been talking about an expensive private school, one that I could never afford on my own.

No problem, he said, *you're family. We help each other out.*

Lately, I've started reading between the lines, and what I see worries me. Tommy went to that same school, and if he was still here, I might not be so concerned.

Things are a lot more complicated now.

There's a coffee bar in the hotel, but I want us to get out into the sun for a bit. We walk to the café where Jade is already waiting for us, waving enthusiastically from her booth. I can feel the smile relax my face. At least something isn't complicated. We've been best friends since college and kept in touch even through my turbulent recent past.

"Jade!" Oliver squeals when he sees her, even though he only remembers her from photos and video chats. When we are close enough, I let go of his hand and he runs to her.

"Olli! You're so big! The last time I saw you in person, you were a baby!"

That is, sadly true. She couldn't make it to the funeral. The last time we saw each other was at Oliver's christening, and after that there never seemed to be an opportunity, but it feels like no time has passed at all. She hugs me too.

"You might have grown an inch or two, but in your case, I think that's the heels," she says after we all sat down. "You look amazing."

"That's a bold-faced lie but thank you. I could use some flattery."

Like the once-over the woman in the lobby gave me earlier? How silly that she's still on my mind. Chances are I'll never see her again.

"I never lie," she returns with some righteous indignation. "How are you? It's been too damn long." She puts her hand to her mouth and giggles, but Oliver has been distracted by the menus the server brought us.

"You're right about that. I'm sorry. I'm really sorry."

To my embarrassment, I can feel my eyes welling up with tears.

She lays a hand on my mine.

"Hey. I understand. You've been through a lot. I wish I could have been there for you in person."

"Your texts and emails helped a lot," I say. It's true. I'm not sure if and how anyone could have done more...and if Rory and Ciara would have let them. *Keep it in the family. This concerns only us.*

Except those times it concerned the Carusos, their sworn enemies, something I believed was, if not a joke, then an exaggeration, until that feud turned deadly.

Too many dark thoughts on the first day of my, our, new beginning.

"This young man here already had lunch, but I'm starving," I say. "Let's order first, and then you have to tell us what you've been up to." Jade was hired by a fashion magazine right out of college, and she's been living her dream ever since.

"I'm starving too," Oliver declares.

"I expected nothing else."

He gives me an indignant, "But Mommy," but he has already made his choice.

I have too, and a few minutes later we sit back and enjoy our food and beverages. Friends, family, without the darker side. I could get used to this.

After the late lunch for me and Jade, afternoon snack for Oliver, we find a park with a playground where he can get all of that sugar out of his system. Me, I feel all right even with some sugar and caffeine in mine, for the first time in many months not bone-tired. Given how early we fled town this morning, I might crash sometime soon, but for the moment, I'm enjoying the difference. Everything is different here.

"You seem...better," Jade observes carefully when we sit on a bench, keeping a close eye on Oliver. "A lot less stressed."

"It's because I am," I admit. "I know they mean well, and the way things are, I have to start looking into preschool. But this school they're talking about, it's a huge decision. Expensive. Far. It would put so much pressure on him..."

"And you?"

"Yeah, that too." I sigh. "I can't help thinking that if I agree to this, I give them all the control."

"And that would be a bad thing."

She doesn't know half of it. Truth be told, I don't know that much more, but once I emerged from the fog, I couldn't ignore my suspicions—or instincts—any longer.

The loss hit them hard too, and I don't even blame them for latching onto Oliver. It's only natural. It has more, graver implications when we're talking about families that are...connected. Is that even the right term for the Flynn family? There's another, harsher one that I haven't been able to acknowledge, yet, or ever.

If I did, I might freak out, and I can't do that to my child. I need to keep it together, stay logical, reasonable.

"It wouldn't be a good thing," I answer. "I get it, they miss Tommy. I do too, but I feel like the long game is to shut me out of every decision concerning my son."

"Do you have proof of that?"

I take in her open, interested expression, trying to gauge how much I can tell her. There's a reason why I'm staying at the hotel, and not with her like she's offered. Even if Rory and Ciara know I'm meeting with her, I don't want her too much on the radar.

What could happen? I'm not sure. But I'm a widow after being married less than two years, through a violent act. I don't particularly feel like taking chances, with my life, or those of the ones I love.

"I have a feeling. To be honest, this is the first time Oliver and I have left town since...it happened."

My throat tightens, and I realize once more I haven't spoken about this much to anyone. Tommy's parents might be just as distraught, but they also have to uphold an image, of strength, of readiness to retaliate.

It's either that, or I'm losing my mind.

"Yes, and that's why I've taken time off to make sure you have a great time while you're here," she promises. "We're going to a museum, cook some great food, and I can watch Oliver for an afternoon too. Something tells me you could use a spa day."

"I don't know. He hasn't been alone with anyone but me or Rory and Ciara."

"Well, he's going to preschool soon, so it's about time that changed," Jade states. "Don't worry, you know I'm the best babysitter you could imagine." She probably has a point, considering that she has three younger siblings.

"Okay. Maybe."

"Great. I assume I can't tempt you with a dip in the pool at my apartment?"

"No," I say, and she leaves it at that.

"That's fine. We can do the museum tomorrow—I know just the place. Oliver is going to love it. And you think about the spa. I'll bring you some brochures. Who knows, you might even go on a date while you're here."

"I doubt it but thank you for having faith in me."

Even the thought seems surreal after my fairy-tale-turned-horror-story relationship. I have too much on my mind. It's true that I miss being with someone, sharing my life with them, the intimacy of it all. I might be ready, if this was just about me, if I didn't have to worry about the role I suspect Rory and Ciara want Oliver to play in the family, and eventually, the family business. Yes, I'm quite certain they are thinking that far ahead.

I have no time to fantasize about a stranger, or even someone more accessible, woman or man. I need to set one foot in front of the other. Going to a museum sounds good, a spa day like an option.

At this point, I come with so many secrets, fears, and half-truths, who would want to put up with that?

Chapter Four

Sienna

Courtney meets with a friend before she returns to the hotel, one of our skilled employees, this one not in the hotel business, reports back to me.

I don't have use for these kinds of methods very often, as the hotel business is my business. I know what lurks under the surface, and I can't be completely ignorant, but the visible parts take up most of my time.

A quick background check on Jade Summers tells me that she's working for the very fashion magazine that's interviewing me tomorrow. Even though it's not her I'm meeting with, this is another red flag. The sooner I get to confront Courtney, the better.

Is it?

As I sit at the desk in my suite, I consider my options and run several scenarios in my mind until I come up with what's the best solution for now.

I'm going to test her.

Given that she's traveling with her son, I doubt that she'll come down to the hotel bar for a drink, so I'll have to employ other strategies. A part of me wants to rush things, go to her room right now and demand an explanation as to why she's in town at this moment.

I'm aware it's not the smartest solution. I'll give it another day or two, see what the reports tell me.

There's another part that can't help wondering, what if it is all a coincidence? I know better than to underestimate anyone from that family, even if she belongs only by marriage. I don't know what she knows. I have to tread carefully.

After dinner I order from the excellent room service—I know it's excellent because I personally worked with the chef on it—I treat myself to another glass of wine, while her picture is still open on my laptop.

Courtney, Tommy Flynn's widow. Who knew she was attracted to women?

—ele—

The report comes in just after I've finished the interview with a writer who's been giving me softball questions, bless her. She's more interested in the design of a Grand Palace suite, and my favorite designers, interior and clothes, than the stories the Flynns have invented surrounding an old incident, and more recently, Tommy Flynn's death.

It's a good thing because I've been more distracted than I care to admit.

Courtney, Jade and Oliver are at the Museum of Natural History, where no doubt the boy will stare in wonder at the dinosaur replica. I wonder if there's any history between the two women as well. College best friends, that could mean so many things.

Not for me, because my path was always carved out for me before I even had any idea what I wanted. I assume it will be similar for Oliver Flynn. Courtney doesn't strike me as the business type, or the person Ciara and Rory Flynn would choose to continue their legacy. Not because she's a woman, but because she's an outsider.

I can relate to that on a certain level. I have no siblings either. Any partner of mine would have to go through a probation period before they could be initiated into the complex business affairs I deal with on a daily basis. Simona and Francesco are lucky. I don't bring anyone home. Not to their house, not to my apartment. The suite is as good as it gets, and I'm fine with that.

Focus is important.

Family is important. Everything else is just a distraction, and I resent Courtney already for being just that.

At the same time, I'm strangely excited to see her again. The possibilities are...intriguing. No surprise that Tommy married her weeks after they met.

It's almost 10 p.m., and I realize I haven't told my aunt and uncle about Courtney's arrival yet.

It doesn't mean anything. I owe them before anyone else, and I sure as hell don't plan to keep anything from them. But maybe there's a chance I can solve this on my own before our planned celebration. I'd prefer it to raising concerns when, perhaps, there's no reason.

Too bad, for me, for her. Under different circumstances, I might have invited her in tonight. The hotel offers an—also excellent—around the clock babysitter service.

The next morning, Courtney doesn't have breakfast at the hotel. Instead, she and Oliver head over to Jade's, where he stays. Courtney comes back out of the apartment building wearing a navy-colored suit and a stressed expression. I have the day off, in theory, since there's always work to do in a business this size. It allows me to take over the surveillance in person.

She walks to the restaurant three blocks down, and when I park the car, I see her go inside and sit at the table with a man her age. That's interesting as well. They hug, but I don't sense any sizzling chemistry between them. Less than with Jade anyway, which tells me this is not a romantic occasion. Usually, I can trust my instincts on this, though I don't find it very reassuring.

It's time to take a closer look.

I go inside as well, not caring now whether or not she sees me. I don't wait for the hostess to assign a place either, just walk to a table close enough to theirs to overhear their conversation and sit.

The hostess comes hurrying after me.

"Ms., please wait a moment..."

"Is this table reserved?" I ask with a cordial smile, taking the wind out of her sails.

"No. A server will be with you in just a moment."

Leaning back in my seat, I direct my attention to the pair two tables away, and I soon realize that I was half right. This is about business. It's not about Rory Flynn's business though. Courtney is looking for a job.

"Thank you so much," she says. "I really appreciate it."

"It's no big deal. I'm afraid though that it's an entry position, so the salary will reflect that."

"I assumed that. I just really need to get out of the house."

"Great. We're all set then. I'll send you the papers."

This is big news. The daughter-in-law, the widow looking for employment outside the Flynn business. What does that mean? Did they kick her out? I wouldn't put it past them. From what I heard about the time our parents were still on speaking terms, no one could ever be good enough for Prince Tommy.

"I'm sorry, but I have to leave now. We'll talk soon. Welcome aboard, Court."

A nickname. That's interesting too. I notice that they had only coffee. This is my opportunity. I wait until he goes to pay the bill at the counter and leaves. As soon as he gets into his car, Courtney gets to her feet and gathers her coat and purse.

She's not going to get away that easily.

I walk the few steps to her table until I'm standing right in front of her, and, conveniently, also blocking her way out.

"Hi. We meet again."

Her eyes widen for a brief, almost imperceptible moment. A beautiful mysterious blue grey. The fact that the situation is serious doesn't mean I can't notice. Paying attention is important in my position. I also noticed that she saw me earlier, so it's not surprise. Guilt? Fear?

She doesn't emanate any of it. Stress is more like it. I could show her ways to relax, but I need to know more before I lay hands on a Flynn. Still, the image lingers.

"We do," she says, sounding like she's barely suppressing a sigh.

Did I misinterpret the signs? No, I decide. I never do. I'm beginning to think that what's on her mind, the reason for her visit, has little to do with the ongoing battle between our families. Or maybe that's wishful thinking, because my treacherous mind is forming ideas, right now, about how this story could continue.

"I haven't had lunch yet," I say, "and from the looks of it, neither have you. Join me, please?"

Now, it's definitely surprise. I know that she must be in her thirties, but damn, she looks young. Harmless? That's yet to be determined. She hesitates.

"I'm Sienna." *But you know that already?*

"Courtney. Courtney Flynn."

23

"I don't believe in coincidences. Would you do me the pleasure?"

I enjoy the soft blush, knowing my choice of words was the right one.

Courtney, clearly flustered, casts a look at her watch. I almost expect her to bolt, but then she says, "Okay, why not. I have a little time before I have to get back."

"Good. A little time is all I'm asking for. What are you in the mood for?"

"I don't know. I didn't plan..."

When the waitress arrives at our table, I order for the two of us, cheese, *courgette* and rosemary pasta, a salad, and wine.

"I wasn't going to..." Again, she lets her words trail off.

"Are you sober?"

She shakes her head.

"Any medical condition? Or pregnant? You don't like wine?"

"No, that's not it. I shouldn't."

I smile at her, and successfully silence her conscience.

"Not good enough a reason?" she asks.

"No. Especially when it's pretty good for the price. Don't worry, I'm not trying to get you drunk. I just wanted to talk to you."

"Why?" That comes out a bit coy. She's caught on.

"Because. It looked like you had a serious business meeting earlier, Courtney Flynn."

She appears unfazed by the non-sequitur, and what if she doesn't have anything to hide?

"A job interview, actually, and I'm lucky I went to school with Will."

"So, you got the job? Now that is a reason to celebrate. Should I have ordered champagne?"

She laughs, the sound of it pleasant, going straight to a place that's inappropriate to think of right now. I need more information first.

"No, it's not that big a deal, but I'm grateful he's giving me the chance. I...You don't want me to dump this on you five minutes after I meet you, but I'm kind of starting over."

I wait until the server has filled our glasses and raise mine in a toast. "To new beginnings, then. Good luck to you, Courtney Flynn."

"Thank you. And just Courtney is fine."

I'm not a particularly sentimental person, but I want to erase that pain from her eyes. Maybe kissing her senseless would do the trick, but we're still in public, and I assume I'm not the only one who has to keep up appearances. None of this sounds like she's on a reconnaissance mission for Rory and Ciara. I can't say for sure yet, but to me, another story emerges: Hanging out with a friend, asking a former classmate for a job, it looks to me like Courtney is cutting her losses, trying to get out from under their influence. It's not easy to be the former spouse in a connected family. I've heard stories. I've seen NDAs signed, and warnings issued.

A worst-case scenario, Sofia Rossi who had to go a long, painful path before she could finally get a divorce from her violent ex. After being named CEO of the Mancini Group, things have been looking up for her. Maybe Courtney's story won't be quite so dramatic. Her husband didn't abuse her. He died, because he was cocky and careless, but I don't want to go down that rabbit hole. Too much discontent and anger between families and former business partners.

We do best when we ignore one another.

It's hard to ignore her though, sitting right across from me, conflicted, desirable.

"Courtney. Sure."

Our food arrives, and I can tell she has no regrets about me having ordered. I watch her take a bite, a sip of wine, her whole demeanor changing as some of that tension finally disappears from her shoulders.

"What about you?" she asks, almost startling me. "Are you here on business, or vacation?"

"Business," I say, watching her closely.

"What kind?"

"Hotels."

"Oh, wow. What a coincidence. I am going to work as a receptionist for Will. He runs a small family hotel and restaurant on the outskirts."

No one's that good an actress, I decide.

"That sounds like an interesting job."

"I actually studied hotel management, a long time ago." She takes another sip, sets the glass down, sighs.

"What happened?"

"I got married. Had a son. Lost my husband."

"I'm so sorry."

"No, I'm sorry. You don't want to hear any of this."

"Whatever you are comfortable sharing," I assure her, and take her hand in mine. That, too, was supposed to be reassurance, but it's electric, all sparks and desire, and when her eyes meet mine, I know it's not just me. What a curious story. Courtney Flynn is running away from home, and I might benefit from that fact in many ways. She might not know much, but perhaps she could shed light on why Rory and Ciara keep holding on to that ridiculous story. Stories. Grief is an explanation, not an excuse.

"In any case, that was two years ago. I can't live at my in-laws' house forever, and I want to find a place to work and live before Oliver goes to pre-school."

"That makes sense."

"Yes, I think it does. I'm afraid they won't be too happy about it...And here I go again. I promise I won't apologize again but thank you for listening when you don't have to. And thank you for suggesting this dish. It's great."

"And the wine?"

"That, too."

When she steals another look at her watch, I'm afraid I'm going to lose her. I can't let that happen. We are both on a tight timetable here.

"I'd like to see you again, Courtney."

Maybe that's a bit bold given what she has just told me. But she has also told me she wants to start over, so I presume we're still on the same page. Her hand still in mine. Courtney isn't new to dating women. I can tell.

"I don't know. At this point, I can't promise much...to anyone."

The regret in her voice is a good sign, I think.

"You got hired. That tells me you are going to stick around for a while. That's enough for me."

The longing in her expression almost causes me pain. There's something we can do about it. Better sooner than later.

Chapter Five

Courtney

Too much, too soon, and it's all so tempting. I haven't felt, or allowed myself to feel this way, in years. I noticed her, and her presence made me nervous for reasons I wasn't ready to acknowledge. I don't know that I am now, but whatever.

When she first stood in front of me, her eyes were steel, and that too had an effect on me. It might be that I'm easy after having denied myself for so long, but there's something about her that makes it impossible to retreat and hide like I have for years.

Those eyes softened when she suggested having lunch, which sounded innocent enough, except that there's nothing innocent about her ordering for me, then touching me in that way...

Sienna, no last name, keeps calling me by my full name for some reason. Her fingers threading through mine are not consoling but igniting. Easy? Maybe. I feel the shiver down my spine, an echo at my core.

It's not something I can set aside or turn off, when it feeds on every curious gaze, every word spoken in that velvety tone. It reminds me of another, almost forgotten life, treacherously promising a different outcome, a future.

I've just met her. There is no future, nothing. I have to consider more than myself, and life is complicated enough already without...what exactly? What are my options?

We have a small argument over the check, and in order to get out of here, and get my head straight—funny—I let her pay.

"I'm sorry. I really have to get back," I say, wishing I didn't blush so easily, her amused smile doing things to me I definitely didn't expect happening when I met Will for that interview. I can't afford to get any more entangled. I want life to be less complicated for a while.

This is why, when she follows me into the alcove at the entrance, partially hidden from the patrons' view, I don't put up the slightest resistance when she pushes me lightly against the wall, her body so close I can feel the heat, and kisses me. I hang on like a person who's drowning, finally offered a lifesaver. Her lips are warm and soft, but the kiss is no gentle ask for permission. She already knows she has it. I imagine I wasn't that hard to read—I've never been. Her hands are on my sides, then move up to my face, anchoring me to her. What's with all the nautical metaphors? Maybe it's because she means danger, tempting, distracting.

"Come with me to my suite," she whispers, her fingers brushing the side of my breast lightly. I can't help gasping, my head spinning with the hot pulse between my legs.

"I can't." I manage to take a step aside, take a deep breath. "I'm sorry, I can't."

It's not that I don't want to. But there's too much on the line.

I flee from the restaurant, almost jogging. She doesn't come after me. I am aware of the faint sense of disappointment as well as the lingering arousal. It would have been so easy.

"You look like you've seen a ghost. Did anything happen?" Jade asks when she opens the door to me. "Your in-laws didn't come after you and forbid you to work outside the house?"

"Too many questions." How is it that I'm still out of breath? "No and no. No ghost either. I just wanted to get out of the rain."

"Yeah. Right."

"There was a bit of rain, earlier."

"Okay, come on in, sit. We're building a giant tower with blocks. Would you like a coffee? A snack?"

My mind is still reeling. I haven't been kissed like that in...forever. Since before Tommy and I moved into his parents' home, and the distance between us kept growing. I don't want to think about this now. New beginnings. I might be a coward, but at least I got the job, that's one item off the list.

"No thanks, I'm not hungry. We had lunch."

"You and Will?" Jade asks. "Off to a good start, then," she comments with a wink.

"Not what you think. We were just catching up."

I had to tell a little white lie, but it's only to protect her. It's best if everyone thinks that I'm only here for a couple of weeks, a long overdue getaway with Oliver, catch up with Jade and an old classmate. Except I pretty much told that witchy woman everything there is to know about me. Mom, married, widowed, trying to make some distance between her and her in-laws. Just got herself a job. Likes men and women. Am I crazy? What possessed me to blurt out all of that?

"It's okay if you don't want to tell me yet," Jade concludes. "I'll hear it eventually."

There's nothing to tell. I walk into the living room where Oliver interrupts his play and comes running.

"Mommy! Look what Jade and I made!"

"Wow," I comment on the indeed giant, colorful construction. "That looks amazing!"

He beams at me, and I wish things could always be that easy. I don't have any illusions about it. He won't always be so focused on me, and eventually he'll ask questions, about Tommy, about his grandparents.

We're not there yet. For the moment, I can protect him from all of it, my own chaotic approach to life, love and dating notwithstanding. A few minutes, and my nerves settle with the blessed familiarity. My son. My best friend. Jade stands by the kitchen island, surveying the scene with a fond smile.

"I think we are looking at an emerging talent," she says. "You two are staying for dinner, right?"

"Can we?"

"Of course," I say, feeling secure and content with my recent decisions.

What if I had extended lunch break a little bit, though? I can't help wondering.

—ele—

There's not much I can do while I'm here, other than what I've already done, meet with Will, get myself a job. I'll start next month, which gives me plenty of time to have that conversation with Rory and Ciara. In the beginning, I can have a room at the hotel, so I'm all set up, nothing left than to obsess about the past and an impossible future, until it all blends together.

Oliver and I stay for dinner, and when he nearly falls asleep during dessert, Jade suggests we could stay overnight. Have some more wine. People don't offer you free wine all the time, so who am I to say no?

Spending time with Jade will delay the inevitable, or so I hope.

When we retreat to the living room with another glass, a sentimental full moon hanging over the city, she says, "I must admit I still don't understand. You really think they could try to take him away from you? I thought you were getting along."

We were, politely, when Tommy was still here. Things were already complicated back then, but at least his presence had a balancing influence, and he trusted me to make the right choices for Oliver.

Because often enough, he wasn't there to make them.

"It's hard to tell," I acknowledge. "Either way, I can't depend on their generosity forever."

"You are family."

Am I?

When Tommy and I first met in a tiny restaurant outside the tourist areas in Lisbon, it seemed like the beginning of a fairy tale. I had just finished grad school and wanted to see the world, or at least a part of it that was far away from home. He had been sent to Europe on business, and for another reason that I wasn't aware of.

Meanwhile, we fell in love, spent time walking along the beach, visited museums, and indulged in delicious seafood and the famous custard tarts. I had a job lined up, but before my return, he took me to Dublin, and then to a romantic cottage the family owns in the countryside. It couldn't have been more romantic.

He proposed on our last night at the cottage, and we returned to the States. He brought back a fiancée, just as his parents wanted. Not Saoirse, though, which made them a lot less excited. She's one of the reasons I knew I had to leave, because there are too many expectations and resentments between me and the Flynn's trusted bodyguard.

I didn't meet her until we came back. I didn't see the signs. I was in love, I was going to get married, and I had my dream job to look forward to. It was so good. Probably too good to be true.

"They helped me with Oliver, sure, but I wasn't the one they wanted for Tommy. I've never been." I fill my glass again, because all of this is in the past, and I need it to stay there. Still, the memory hurts. Always wondering about Saoirse, especially when I realized how hard his death hit her. It was more, much more than the idea that someone could call her professional reputation into question, especially when she wasn't with him that night.

The first two months were married bliss, and then we moved in with his parents. It wasn't a suggestion, it was expected. Stay close to the business and the family, and Saoirse.

"Anyway," I continue. "I'll talk to them, find out what they really want." Or I'll just rip off the band-aid and never go back. The furniture, the clothes, I could leave it all behind and start over. Much of it doesn't belong to me anyway.

"That's probably the best solution."

Two months, and the man I had shared so much with, whose curiosity and laughter had drawn me to him, became a stranger. He worked long hours, and he never shared anything about the details of his day. Import, fine whiskey and other liquors.

Meeting with scary, tight-lipped men every once in a while. Making an unbelievable amount of money. It wasn't until the police came to the house after the shooting that I'd heard those harsher words. Connected families. Organized crime. I overheard one of the cops use the term mobster. He thought I wasn't paying attention, and for too long, I didn't. The female FBI agent was more polite. She left her card as well, imploring me to call should I need anything. She, too, used those terms.

I didn't want to believe it at first, but the more I think about it, the more it looks like the missing link. Now I wonder if they were trying to turn me, but how? I didn't know a thing about the business, had nothing to give them. The truth?

I still don't know, and probably never will, if Tommy meant to protect Oliver and me, or if he simply didn't care to fill me in on the finer details.

But now it makes sense why a man running a family business needs this much security. Why a member of a feuding family would murder him in an alley.

Maybe it's grief and loneliness that made me paranoid, but I've decided I prefer to be safe than sorry. Oliver is all I have, and if only a sliver of my speculations, fears, is true, then I can't have him grow up in these surroundings.

I don't want him to become the heir.

I'm afraid of losing him too, and I don't think I could handle it.

Chapter Six

Sienna

Simona and Francesco greet me the way they always do, like they haven't seen me in forever. I've had enormous luck out of trauma, family that stepped in when my parents were killed in a car accident. I was five years old. My aunt and uncle didn't hesitate and raised me as their own.

They made sure a traumatized child wasn't only fed and clothed but loved. And beyond.

With my parents gone, they were next in line, and they also assumed their responsibilities in the business, responsibilities I'd later share, that one day will be mine only. They prepared me well for that, with the best schools and universities, and sky-high expectations.

Perhaps I learned to associate that love with fulfilling those expectations, with unquestioning loyalty to our family.

Because family is all you have, and I know better than anyone else what it's like to have that ripped away from you, abruptly and brutally. That was a long time ago, when my grandfather and Rory Flynn's father used to smoke cigars and sample that fine whiskey, before one of those bottles nearly killed a Grand Palace hotel guest. Or so I've been told.

I wrench my mind away from the tales of the past and give both of them a quick hug.

"Come on in, Sienna." Francesco lays an arm around my shoulders. "Simona has been cooking up a storm. We wanted to properly welcome you."

"You didn't have to..." It's futile. I get treated to a feast at a regular family dinner. Coming home after securing all those new developments, I knew she'd go all out.

I have a glass of champagne in my hand before I'm fully out of my coat.

"Tell us," Francesco says, "Did they ask a lot of questions? About that time?"

No one's holding anything back.

"No," I say. "Our record speaks for itself. They know it was a singular incident, and they know who created all the chaos surrounding it. They're excited to be in business with us."

"Great, great. I never doubted you could do it."

That's right, though a complete lack of doubt can be frightening too. You must make it come true every time.

─ele─

We talk about the meetings, and Simona asks me about the interview. I excelled there, too, no surprise, no doubt.

I sit up straighter when they mention Courtney, the woman who left me standing in a haze of lust, caught me off guard there for a second when I thought I had her where I wanted her.

"Flynn has his house in disarray," Francesco says with unveiled disgust. "He's one to talk, when he got his son killed, and apparently, his daughter-in-law has run away."

"She has?" I ask, keeping my tone neutral. I still remember the taste of her lips, the way she felt under my hands. Promising. Eager. I suppress a sigh as he continues,

"Took the boy with her too. Doesn't look like it was in their plan. Silly people, they are dreaming of the day when he takes over already. I don't wish a man dead for no reason, but they gave him far too much leeway. Too much freedom is a dangerous thing."

I ponder his words, the meaning between the lines, and I decide I don't like what I'm hearing. Tommy Flynn's flaws aside, I'm not sure I would agree to a partner of their choice. An arranged marriage, like Mia Leonard and Alessandra Falcone.

Oh well, I haven't heard of a divorce. They keep to themselves and seem happy, and that's all that matters. It might work for some people. It sure wouldn't work for me, and apparently it didn't for Tommy Flynn.

But perhaps they're just insulting his choice, and I resent that too. What is this? She's a stranger to me. I have known Simona and Francesco all my life, so why would I feel the need to defend her?

"Whatever her intentions are, I don't think it has anything to do with us."

"Unless Rory wants to blame that on us too. But you're right, let's forget about them," Simona says. "We are so proud of you, Sienna. One day this will all be yours, and it didn't just fall in your lap, no, you earned it."

"I'm happy to drink to that," I reply, and they laugh. I take a hasty sip. Some of my unease remains, reminding me that nothing can ever be easy.

If there's anything Rory can come up with to blame us for the latest developments, he sure will.

Meanwhile, my curiosity and my completely irrational hunger for her won't let me be.

"I'm sorry," I say, getting to my feet. "I need to make one more work call."

Chapter Seven

Courtney

I'm standing in the grand entrance hall of the Flynn mansion, the place I've called home for the past four years. An exaggeration. A misinterpretation, maybe.

It's dark, and a sound makes me spin around, my breath catching in my throat when I see the dark figure stepping out of the shadows. One of the men who came to Tommy's office, whose names I never learned.

He's holding a gun. I want to scream, but no sound comes out.

"Traitor," he scoffs and raises his weapon. I think of Oliver sleeping upstairs, of Tommy going out in that alley, a sound, and the world turns black...

I wake with a start, my heart racing. In the bed next to me, Oliver is still sound asleep. I hear footsteps and laughter from the hallway, other guests returning.

I might have run away from home, but the nightmare has followed me here too, rooted in the fear that history inevitably repeats itself. My PJs are clinging to my skin, and I shiver.

I'm afraid it might all be true, and there was never again a safe place from the moment I married Tommy Flynn.

_ℓℓ_

I'm halfway, anxiously back to sleep when the phone rings. I pick up quickly as to not to wake Oliver, and sure enough, it's her voice calming my nerves like a warm embrace. She's doing something else to my nerves too, sure, but for now I'm happy to chase the cobwebs of the nightmare from my mind. I carefully get out of bed and tiptoe to the bathroom.

Then something else springs to mind.

"How did you get this number?"

"From your papers on the table, at the restaurant," she says, making no apology for spying on my personal information. "I told you I wanted to see you again."

"Um…okay." It's strange and excitingly intimate, talking to her with only the soft light of the lamp over the mirror.

"Do you want to?" she asks bluntly. "I got the feeling you might be interested."

"Oh…I am." What the hell am I doing? "I mean…I'm sorry for running out on you. Things are a bit complicated right now." And if they are as complicated as I suspect, I should wait until I've had that talk with Rory and Ciara or decided to go underground all together. I suppress a nervous laugh. Is this real? Are the same people who killed Tommy really going to come after me? Are my in-laws? Am I losing my mind? "I'm not feeling too well, to be honest."

"New beginnings can be hard," she says sincerely. "But maybe we can find a way to make you feel better. My suite is 701. Meet me tomorrow at noon. I'll clear my afternoon."

"Another lunch date?" I'm tempting fate and I know it. We weren't on a date. We're two strangers who, after encountering each other twice, nearly made out in a hallway, and it felt so good. She's not wrong to assume I want more. And given that in a few days from now I'll have to face the consequences of my actions, build a new life with my son, or go on the run for real...Why not?

"If you will."

I can hear the smile in her voice, and it makes me smile too. A bit nervous. Excited in a way I haven't been in years.

"Good. I happen to know you make excellent choices."

"I know. I'll see you at noon. Don't be late."

"I never..." She's gone already, and I stare at the phone, bemused, feeling like I imagined this entire conversation. Her number in my recently received calls is real though. I save it and type her name next to it. Sienna.

Let's see what else you're good at.

Switching gears hard, I step over to Oliver's bed. Nightmares, late night tempting calls, he blissfully slept through all of it.

"I'll never do anything to hurt you," I whisper. "You're the most important person in my life."

I will always protect my son. And I deserve to have a little secret, something that's just my own.

⁓

In the morning, after I get both of us ready for breakfast, I ask, "Would you like to spend the day with Jade again? Mommy has something to take care of."

"Yes! Jade is nice. I like her." That was easier than I expected, and I shouldn't question it. Given my plans, I shouldn't be jealous that Oliver likes spending time with someone other than me.

I can do this.

I call Jade whom we were going to meet again tomorrow and take a deep breath.

"Could I ask you a favor?"

"Anything, sweetie," she says. "You know that."

"Okay. I know we've been taking up a lot of your time lately, and I swear I'll make it up to you, but could you watch Oliver again today? I have to—"

"Of course!" she interrupts me. "He's a cutie. We can have dinner again? I'm going to show you one of my favorite Vegan restaurants in the area. You'll love it. Wait...You're seeing Will again, aren't you?"

Jade knows that I had been dating men and women before my marriage, but I don't blame her for her interpretation.

"No, I'm not. I thought I'd do that spa day like you suggested. They even have coupons here at the hotel."

The latter part is not a lie, the rest...I'll have a lot to make up for eventually. And I will. Once I have the rest figured out, once I have dared to go down that road just one time.

"Like I said, it's no problem. I might be a little disappointed it's not a hot date, but hey, you could use a bit of pampering after everything you've been through."

I can't help laughing, relief, nerves, all of it. "Is that a nice way of telling me I need to improve my appearance?"

"No, silly. That's my way of telling you that you deserve all of it. Olli and I will have a lot of fun."

"Thank you." My mood takes a harsh swing, and I can feel my throat tighten. Nothing will be easy in the coming months. It's good to have a friend.

"You're welcome. Are you coming over now?"

"We'll just have breakfast, and then...I think yes."

I can't be late. I promised. But before that lunch date, I need to make a purchase.

We don't have lunch when I enter Sienna's suite at the Grand Palace, at least not right away. Part of me knew, because I didn't come back here for her exquisite taste in food though that doesn't harm. The moment I step over the threshold, and her eyes rake over me in that intimate, possessive way, reality, the possibility of danger, my fears for the future, it all falls away.

"You look gorgeous," she says, brushing her hand over my cheek, and I'm happy I had the foresight to do a bit of shopping. The red dress seems to be to her liking, and I hope what's underneath it will be too.

"Look who's talking," I return, eliciting a knowing smile. She's not self-conscious at all, and I wasn't exaggerating. Her outfit is the kind of sexy business wear you can hide under a blazer until it's time for an intimate dinner.

And then rational thought vanishes when she leans in, and our lips meet again. I have been breathlessly waiting for this, from the moment I left Jade's, the time spent in the store trying to find the perfect clothes for this afternoon delight, including lingerie. I didn't expect to go out with anyone here, let alone have the need for lingerie, but this is where we are.

She kisses me deeply, and this time I don't hesitate or falter, but kiss her back with the same passion, my hands fumbling for the zipper of her dress while hers cup my breasts, her touch warm through the thin layers of fabric, my nipples hardening with the sensation.

I have been here less than five minutes, and I'm moaning. She must be thinking I'm...What, easy? Desperate? If she does, Sienna doesn't seem to mind, and that's good enough for me.

We don't have forever. No one does, I learned that the hard way. So, we make the best of the time we have.

I finally succeed, and with a soft sound, her dress falls to the floor. There's a hint of surprise in her smile, as if she didn't expect me to be so bold.

There's a bit more to my story than most people imagine.

"I'm glad you changed your mind." She steers me towards a double door, and the bedroom. I take a moment to admire the suite. It's huge, likely double the size of my room which wasn't on the cheap side.

"Getting distracted?"

My focus is back on her when she runs a hand down my back, and lower, and the next moment, I'm on my back, Sienna on top of me, and I don't mind at all. I have always enjoyed letting a more mature partner take the lead, women in particular, and I'm happy to do it now.

The world becomes a blur of lust and sensation as she sits back to take the dress off me, then the lacy bra and panties, and kisses me again. I hold her to me, pressing against her, not caring anymore if I come off as needy or desperate. That's because I kind of am, every heartbeat intensifying the pulse between my legs. She indulges me for a few moments, and then I draw a sharp breath when she moves lower down my body to brush her tongue over my nipple, every muscle tightening at my core.

This is what it feels like to be free. I had almost forgotten. And it's not over yet. I squirm and shiver under her gentle but firm touch, eager for more, and Sienna gives me more, hot kisses, the tease of her fingertips. When she leans in for a taste, I don't even care about the undignified sound coming out of my mouth. I am amazed, grateful, stunned that this is real, not a pointless fantasy that will never come true.

Her hands tighten on my hips, and I close my eyes and let go. I forgot how much this feels like flying when it's just right.

—ᘒᘒ—

I am eager to reciprocate, and Sienna doesn't have any objections at all. It's a relief, too, to let the mask fall, to finally touch her the way I wanted to pretty much from the beginning. That's not despair or coincidence. It's that sheer luck you don't often have in life. Chemistry. Whatever it is, it works both ways. She's quieter, but leaving her gasping, with a racing heart, fills me with a sense of pride. I don't know Sienna well, but I can already tell she doesn't let her guard down very often, and she doesn't let a lot of people close. Likes to stay in control.

Making her lose control comes with a sense of pride.

Her smile tells me that she sees right through me.

"Reminiscing?" she asks, satisfaction audible in her voice. It wakes my body with a start.

"I don't know, it all just happened. I very much remember," I say as I prop myself up on my elbow, studying her.

"You are adorable and funny. I think I'll keep you around for a while."

"That's all you have to say about me?"

"Well, since you ask…" Her voice drops to a sensual murmur. "Sexy." Sienna traces a finger down my spine, and I couldn't suppress the shiver if my life depended on it. "Insatiable," she comments. "I like that, too, about you."

"I'm glad. Because it's not going to change anytime soon."

"Hm. You're hungry?" She leans over and places kisses where her finger has been.

Only the tiniest move, and the friction of the sheet against my skin produces results.

"Very much," I confess.

"Good." She brushes my hair aside and leans in to kiss my neck, and I melt into her embrace as her hands take more liberties, one of them sneaking between my legs. I am ready.

Chapter Eight

Sienna

When I order room service, it's a little after two, and I know without a doubt that while possibly reckless, I made the right decision. I had the right instincts about Courtney too, knowing that making a move would be worth it, that there's likely more to her story than the occasional college experiment.

There are many tricky implications mixed into this, but I have no regrets for the time being. It might have a little to do with my aunt and uncle badmouthing someone they've never met, only because of her association with Rory and Ciara. Loose association, I'm pretty certain. They don't know she applied for a job, wouldn't approve of it either. Not that I care, not now when we are waiting for the food while she's still wrapped in the sheet, a fond smile on her face.

I have dressed to answer the door, and because at some point, the intimacy of lying in each other's arms is too much, too dangerous for what, for who we are.

Even giving Courtney the benefit of the doubt, assuming that she still has no idea who I am.

There was a moment, when she nodded off with my arms around her, that I entertained the idea of telling her. I have no idea where that came from. This is an indulgence, giving in to an impulse. We'll see how long it lasts.

There's a knock on the door, and I tear my gaze away to go and answer.

"Thank you, I got it from here."

All of my employees are thoroughly vetted and loyal, but I can't take the chance that one of them finds Courtney Flynn in my bed.

Smiling to myself, I think even given her rocky relationship to the Flynns, it's probably the most subversive thing I've ever done in my life—and there have been a few.

When I wheel the cart into the room, Courtney comes out of the bedroom, now fully dressed again. She watches me take the dome lids off with a bemused smile.

"Are you ever going to let me take a look at menus?" she asks.

I know it's a joke, but somehow it bothers me. I imagine Tommy Flynn made a lot of decisions for her, whether he wanted to or not. His parents would demand it. It's a dilemma all right. I understand that there's a need for some of those demands. Playing the role can be exciting. Sometimes it just plain sucks.

"In my defense, there's a bit of everything," I say. "But yes, the next time you can choose from the menu."

"I was kidding. This looks great." She looks up at me, her eyes widening. I could get lost in them. Dangerous indeed, even if she doesn't know it. "There's going to be a next time?"

"Of course. I know you have to go back sometime, and I think we've established that meeting again would be...beneficial."

"I like those benefits," she says as she takes a strawberry from one of the plates and puts it into her mouth.

At this rate, I might just not let her go.

Courtney leaves after coffee and dessert. Being alone in the suite with work to do sobers me up—to some extent. I have some more coffee, take care of the day's business, make calls, assure myself that everything's going as planned with the new developments.

So far, Courtney's presence hasn't raised red flags with my investigator. She does what she says she'd do, activities with her son, the two of them hanging out with Jade some more. She calls her ex-classmate, soon-to-be-boss one time. They make an appointment for her to come out to her future workplace and temporary home.

She doesn't call her old home, her in-laws, once.

She has agreed to meet me for dinner, and given how the last few days went, I see nothing wrong with taking her to one of the hotels' restaurants, not here in the city, but at one of our resorts in the country.

Great for hiking, golf, all kinds of outdoor sports.

I doubt we'll spend much time outside.

Chapter Nine

Courtney

Falling for an attractive, charming, and kind man during my first vacation overseas, that was me. I can't bring myself to have any regrets, because what we had at one time was real.

Even when that chasm appeared between us and we grew further apart during our time at the mansion, he was still kind, a devoted father to Oliver.

Having a secret affair with my best friend's father's second ex-wife before I met Tommy, that was also me. I don't know if Jade ever found out, and I never dared ask if she knew, but as I sit in the cab on the way to her apartment, I can't help feeling grateful for Diana Wynter, who took me out of the realm of crushing on more mature women without ever doing anything about it. Of course, back then, it didn't take all that much to be more mature than I was.

I'd like to think it's different now, that Sienna and I are on more equal footing, given the serious experiences I've had in the past few years, and yet...The excitement is the same, no, even more intense now. I wish I could say there's no need to hide, but that will only be temporary, until I've figured things out.

I have not heard from Rory or Ciara, which is a good thing. Perhaps it won't be so hard to understand that I need to stand on my own two feet. If they were worried about any secrets coming out, well, I wasn't privy to them in the first place.

Chances are, they are just as relieved to see me go as I am to leave, and it doesn't mean they won't get to see Oliver. He loves them, and if it's at all possible, I'd prefer to keep them in his life, as long as they can acknowledge that I'm his mother, and they can't dictate Oliver's future.

A few days away have already given me a new perspective, or maybe it was the few hours I spent with Sienna. Will I see her again? I don't know. I need to keep my focus, settle into a new life, a new job, a new home with my son.

Do I *want* to see her again? Absolutely. Everything about her intrigues me. Sitting in the restaurant with her, talking, had me spell-bound. Sex with her has me hooked. She's just so different from anyone I've ever met, from the people that surrounded me for most of my life.

It's hard to explain, but when I arrived here, I was feeling so tired and dispirited. Guilty even.

Now I'm certain that there is a life out here for me. It's not just an illusion.

Jade is discreet as long as Oliver is still listening attentively to our conversation, but when we have coffee and dessert while he's watching one of his favorite shows on the couch, she doesn't hold back.

"Okay, spill it. You don't glow like this from a day at the spa."

"You think? The massage was extraordinary."

It was, and I nearly fell asleep when she treated me to it. Even now, I can't remember the last time I felt so deeply relaxed. Certainly not since moving in with Tommy's parents and trying to pretend there was nothing strange about the arrangement, that family and their business, or the people coming and going.

Nothing strange about the police thinking my husband's murder wasn't a tragic isolated incident, but a hit on a well-known figure in organized crime. I shudder, thinking it's close to a miracle they believed my righteous indignation. I didn't lie. I had no idea what they were talking about, and I couldn't imagine that he was involved in any of the things they suggested. Even the FBI knocked on our door one time. At that point, Rory was threatening to sue, something the investigators acknowledged with nothing more than a shrug.

When they left, their visits becoming sparser over time, I had Oliver to take care of. I had to overcome my own shock at the same time, and there was no way I could have played detective. Maybe I should have tried?

"Courtney, honey, I'm losing you. Trip down memory lane?"

"Sorry," I say with a sigh. "Yes. My mind sometimes takes me there without warning."

"Let's take it back here, then." She heads over to the fridge, takes out a bottle and pours an Irish cream liquor on ice for both of us. "We'll get the truth out of you yet."

"I thought we already had dessert...Okay, okay. You were right. I didn't go to the spa."

"I knew it!" Jade nearly squeals, and I put a finger to my lips, but Oliver is still immersed in his show. "You must tell me all about him. Her? Them?"

"Her. She. At least I'm pretty sure though we didn't raise the question." I can't hold back the smile, making her chuckle.

"I see. You were busy with other subjects."

"Jade. Please."

"I'm really happy for you. How did you meet her?"

So, I tell her that Sienna was in the hotel lobby when I arrived, and that she happened to be in the same restaurant where I had lunch with Will. I nearly give myself away and tell her about the job interview, too, but catch myself at the last moment. It's too early for that. I also leave out details about the afternoon and how exactly Sienna blew my mind. It's never going to be the right time to share that with another soul. Judging by the way my face heats when I circumvent the subject, Jade is likely guessing.

"Wow, that's pretty amazing. So, you're going to see her again?"

"I think so," I say. Apparently, I've made progress since the cab ride, because this feels right. Real. At least this time I didn't run out on her.

Whatever comes out of this, it's exciting. I've missed this.

I look over to where Oliver is about to fall asleep, and I'm getting extremely far ahead of myself, but I wonder if she'd like to meet him.

I am feeling too good to think clearly about anything at the moment.

———

However, I don't suggest it when I call her that night, again in the bathroom, this time not after a nightmare, but just because I want to.

"I wish you were here," she says, her words laden with meaning and sexy insinuations.

"I wish that too, but I needed a bit of time to catch my breath," I admit. Not just metaphorically.

"I see. Lots of exercise today."

"That too. It was pretty amazing though." I see no harm in admitting the truth.

"That means you'll go away with me on the weekend?"

"I want to. I really do—"

"If you're worried about Oliver, bring him, and I promise you I can hire a babysitter service of the highest quality you can imagine."

"I don't know. Between my in-laws and Jade, he hasn't been with strangers much..."

"The offer stands," she says warmly. "That, or I'll reimburse Jade accordingly. They appear to have a good bond, and I'm fine with that if it eases your mind."

Something about this suggestion strikes me as strange—what exactly is she talking about, reimbursing Jade? And when did I tell her Oliver's name?

All I can say is, "You'd do all that just so I go away with you? Why?"

"Because I like you, Courtney," she says as if it's the most reasonable explanation. "I like being with you, and I'm in the position to make that happen—if you want."

"I...yes. Of course." Flustered doesn't even begin to cover it. The way she speaks, the way she holds herself...the way she lets go...I want to be with her too, as much as I possibly can. Everything right now is so fragile, the idea that someone could be in it with me, someone like her, is intoxicating. She has already given me more than she'll ever know.

"So, then, talk to Jade. We'll have dinner at the Grand Palace resort, and we'll stay in the river suite afterwards."

"Another suite. You rent that one too, just in case?"

"No," she says with a laugh. "I was going to wait for you to say yes."

"That's...considerate. Thank you. I'll talk to Jade."

"I was hoping you'd say that," she whispers. "So, dinner, drinks and then..."

The last part of her sentence makes me blush again, even though it's just me alone in the dark. I'm hopeless. I also have hope again for the first time in a long time.

Chapter Ten

Sienna

I love my job. The official one, my family's pride, running the ever-expanding group of hotels and resorts. There's a lot of work in it, and a lot of rewards. With those come some aspects I could do without, but they're part of the package, had been long before I was born.

I have learned that there's no point in raising my concerns with Francesco, Simona, or any of my cousins. Especially not the cousin who was in the bar that night drinking with Tommy Flynn. They think we consider ourselves better than them, and it makes them mad, even though it's not even real. We have no time to be snobs, we have a business to run, and Mr. and Mrs. Flynn would do well to focus on theirs. Nico hung out with Tommy a few times in the "between," precarious, but not as dangerous as things became once Flynn stepped out in that alley and got himself shot over some botched deal. Drugs, weapons, I don't know, and I don't want to.

Our family appreciates art. It pairs well with the official part, and we don't contribute to the deaths of a substantial part of the population. Like I say, I never found out what exactly happened that night, and neither did Nico, though he's been in Europe ever since, putting distance between him and overzealous authorities, and the vengeful Flynns.

I'm more relieved than ever when the workday is finally over, all parts of it taken care of, and I can move on to something more uplifting, planning my weekend with Courtney.

I can tell I startled her a bit by mentioning paying Jade for her babysitter services, which makes me think I need to take the leap and tell her something soon.

I'm still testing her. It's not like she has anything to take home to the Flynns, because then she'd have to admit that she's been sleeping with the enemy. No, I don't think she has any interest in that.

Rory and Ciara might plan to be around and be grandparents. That could become a problem if we run into each other.

Not now, not this weekend.

I call the resort and book a suite on the top floor, with the river view as promised. It's outfitted similarly to the local Grand Palace, with a few more amenities, a bigger pool, and all-inclusive options. But since I'm the boss, it will be all-inclusive anyway for Courtney.

We are back on track. Because of my hard work in the past years, no one talks about the Flynns' accusations any longer, or maybe they're just busy picking up the pieces, not being that business savvy to begin with. I'm going to be on the cover of a freaking fashion magazine.

I think I deserve to treat myself. It doesn't change my loyalty to Francesco and Simona, or my dedication to the business generations before us built.

I'm not looking for a fairy tale romance, but Courtney happened to be in the right place at the right time, and I plan to take advantage in every way I can. For her pleasure and mine.

Satisfied with all the preparations, I look up Jade Summers' number and call her.

This should be easy.

———eee———

Before the weekend, I check in with my aunt and uncle to make sure there will be no surprises. I might tell them sometime, if this gets mildly serious, or never at all. Time will tell. For now, as long as things are working according to plan, there's no need.

Courtney texts me that Jade will watch Oliver for the time we'll be gone, but she has to be back on Sunday as her former friend and boss-to-be will pick her and Oliver up to take them to their new home.

She still hasn't contacted her in-laws, according to the reports I get on a regular basis.

Better that way.

I'll have a little over twenty-four hours with her, and I plan to make them count.

———eee———

I instruct the driver to go to Jade's apartment building where I slip inside when another tenant leaves and take the elevator up to her floor. It's a fairly wealthy neighborhood though I doubt anyone will recognize me here. I knock on the door, and Jade opens it to me, poker face in place. Everybody needs something, don't they? Courtney has been keeping secrets from her best friend, but the same is true vice versa.

Courtney joins us a moment later, her expression turning guarded when she sees me. That is no surprise either. I'm sure she thought I was going to wait downstairs.

"Hi, Courtney. Are you ready?"

Before she can answer, the boy comes running into the room, stopping cold when he notices the stranger in the room.

"Hi," I say as I crouch down in front of him. "I'm Sienna, your mom's friend. You must be Oliver."

He nods empathically. "Yes, but you can call me Olli."

"Oh, thank you. Olli it is. I hope you don't mind I'm taking her away for a bit. She'll be home before you know it."

"Jade and I are going to bake a cake," he tells me.

Courtney's expression is downright stormy now. "You'll be nice for Jade, okay? I'll be back soon." She picks him up and holds him close for a moment before she lets him down again. "Let's go."

"Bye, Olli. Jade. Leave us some of that cake, will you?"

He stares at me in awe. Jade isn't so easily impressed, but the corner of her mouth twitches.

Assured that everything is taken care of, I brace myself.

Courtney sulks all the way down to the street, where the driver puts her suitcase into the trunk, and we settle into the backseat.

"That wasn't cool," she finally says.

"Me meeting your son? Why, you wanted me to be your dirty little secret?" I ask, amused.

"No!"

"Then what is the problem?"

"You could have waited. I didn't even know you wanted to meet him and I...I don't know, I could have prepared for it better. I haven't dated anyone in years. Oliver doesn't remember Tommy much, and I never introduced..." She lets her words trail off, frustrated, and I feel a sliver of guilt creep in.

Courtney does have a point.

"I'm sorry. You're right, I should have asked you first."

She sighs, can't help the smile that's forming. "Which is not your strong suit as I've learned."

"True. If you can't forgive me yet, well...I'll think of ways to make you in the next twenty-four hours."

The way her breath catches makes me think it won't take that long. Content that she won't hold my actions against me—this particular action anyway—I lean back in my seat.

"So, we're dating now?"

"Aren't we? Otherwise, what is it we are doing?" she asks, curiosity mixed with frustration in her tone.

I plan to satisfy both. Soon. I'd love to make it look like I have all the power here, but the thought of having her underneath me, naked, again, makes me weak in the knees.

I'm good at compartmentalizing, and that helps. Everything regarding the business is taken care of, and even though I'm always on call when it comes to emergencies, we should be undisturbed for the next few hours. This whole set-up, the driver, picking one of our resorts, of course it's about control. It matters to me, more so because of her background, but it would even if she wasn't still using his last name. At the same time, I'm aware of how much I've been looking forward to this day, the time with her, which is unsettling to say the least.

"We're adults. It is whatever we want it to be," I give her the answer. It might be a copout, but she doesn't question it.

We stop on the way for a coffee and snack because dinner will be late. Courtney's eyes light up when she talks about her son, and they grow somber and sad when the subject of conversation moves to her late husband. I don't interject much, just listen, trying to understand how she got mixed up with the family.

A chance meeting in Lisbon, a romantic week in the Irish countryside, a short honeymoon phase before everything changed. Courtney doesn't go into details, but it's easy to tell she's been searching for answers, why a businessman would be murdered in an alley. Having those answers would help all of us, I think. We won't be friends ever again the way it apparently was generations ago, something that Tommy and Nico tried to revive in a short-lived and futile attempt—but it would help a lot if the Flynns kept their noses out of our business. In return, we might be able to stop keeping an eye on them.

A fantasy.

"I am talking too much. Again," Courtney says ruefully. "Here I am on a date—I think—with an amazing mysterious woman, and all I can talk about is my late husband and my in-laws. I'm so sorry."

"I'll take amazing, thank you. Mysterious, not so much, I'm afraid. And I don't mind you talking about all of this. It was a traumatic loss."

She looks lost for a moment. "I guess it was," she finally says, and even though we're in public, I reach out and brush my fingers over her cheek, eliciting a soft smile. Soft. Warm. That describes Courtney well, though she has an edge to her, and an air of danger mixed in with the naivete that draws me to her. She's on the edge of discovery.

We need to talk. This discovery could have far-reaching consequences for both our families.

But first, delicious food and mind-blowing sex. All hell might break loose at some point, and why not enjoy ourselves first?

When we arrive, I watch with pride as she takes in the surroundings, awe in her expression. This is what I want all guests to feel like when they stay in one of our resorts but seeing the emotion on Courtney's face makes it special. I loved this place when I first set eyes on it, and we made it even more spectacular. The lobby bar is both cozy and elegant. We reach the highest floor with the suites in a smooth elevator ride, and when we walk to our door, we get a glimpse of the gardens and spas facing the river. The view...it's not free, but at the same time, it's priceless.

I'm sure Courtney has seen plenty of luxurious accommodations during her marriage, but she hasn't lost the wonder.

I am satisfied with how my plans are going, but moments from now, it will be even better.

⁓ℓℓ⁓

All hell breaks loose sooner than I imagined, and when it does, I consider it a good thing that Courtney can't go anywhere. Between the conversation I had with Jade, and taking Courtney out of town to the resort, there's still a chance to figure this out.

Chapter Eleven

Courtney

It's unreal. For years, I've felt so alone, so trapped in a foreign environment, seeing no way out. Yes, I could talk to Jade every once in a while, but I couldn't imagine asking her to come over or leaving the mansion. It just didn't occur to me.

And I certainly couldn't share my suspicions and concerns with Rory and Ciara, when according to them, Tommy walked on water.

Especially after the police came to the house.

Once they stopped coming around, the subject that any part of the business could be less than legal was never again raised in the house.

And who was I to question it? I had no clue about any of it. I didn't sign the bills. Protected. Shut out.

With Sienna, it's so different. I don't tell her about my suspicions either, but I'm starting to feel that maybe someday, I could. She's an excellent listener. No one has given me this much room to give voice to my feelings in forever, and it feels so good. Even better knowing what's in the near future for us.

The river suite. Hours of glorious oblivion before we go back home, and I start to confront real life. Ciara sent me a text this morning.

When are you coming home? We miss you and the little man.

I haven't answered yet, because once I do, I can't hide the truth any longer. I doubt that they miss me, but that's beside the point.

In the suite, we are all over each other, obsessed, the moment the door closes. I can't get enough of her hands, knowing my body intimately, her mouth on mine.

Sienna steps away, catching her breath, her smile stealing mine. I might as well be naked already, my heart racing, my mind dominated by helpless desire.

"I'll be right back," she promises. "I just have to talk to someone at reception."

Without further explanation, as if she hadn't been about to ravish me in the middle of the room just seconds ago, she walks away.

Trying to relax, I take out my phone and check my messages. Ciara again.

Let's have a nice dinner out when you come back. We need to talk, don't you think?

She has no idea.

Jade has sent a message too, a couple of selfies of her and Oliver joking around, and another photo. I read the caption first, then click on the image, and within seconds, my heartbeat accelerates again, not in a good way this time. I stare at it, my fingers clutching the phone growing numb.

Is that your Sienna? Looks like she owns the place you're staying at.

It's the cover of a magazine soon to be released.

Hotel Tycoon Sienna Caruso Answers All says the headline.

What the hell is going on? What is she doing?

The thought of various worst-case scenarios jolts me into action.

Is everything okay? I ask Jade, and she answers right away.

Yes, of course. We're fine. Enjoy your stay.

She doesn't know, of course, because I never told her everything that's been said about the Caruso family behind closed doors at the mansion. How Nico Caruso was a murderer and a cheat, and the whole family covered for him. A policeman saw someone that fit his description, though they could never get to him. The authorities, that is. Now I'm wondering if Rory was actually talking about sending someone after him. Retaliation? Vendetta?

I'm dizzy with anger and fear. Sienna has been playing with me, I could live with that. I don't take well to people who put my son's life in danger.

Rory, Ciara, Sienna, her cousin, I don't give a damn. I just want peace.

I take my purse and my unopened suitcase and open the door.

She's standing in front of me, giving a surprised laugh.

"Going somewhere? Already?"

I hold up the phone, so she can see the photo on the screen. Her expression gives nothing away.

"Why should I stay here a minute longer, Ms. *Caruso*?"

Sienna isn't even shocked or surprised I found out. That makes me even madder at her.

"What the fuck?" It's hard to find the words when my world is crumbling underneath me—again—but those seem fitting. "What did you do? I need to get my son! Don't touch me!" I yell as she gently steers me further back into the room and closes the door. She's still so damn calm.

"Okay," she says quietly.

"Are you crazy? Nothing about this is remotely okay. Oliver..."

"He's safe with Jade and you know that. He's a child. He has nothing to do with any of it. Why would I want to harm him?"

"Yes, why. Indeed." She makes a good point, but I can't trust her any longer, and I wanted to, so much. "Because he's Tommy's son. Because your people got him killed?"

"Courtney."

"No!" I can't stand this, the way she tries to reason with me, calm me, as if I didn't have the right to be completely out of my mind, after what she called a traumatic loss. It doesn't stop being traumatic when everyone around me is lying. And all of a sudden, I'm sobbing. Anger is still a part of it, embarrassment sneaking in, but I'm unable to stop it now that the floodgates have opened. I need to get out of here, and so I make another weak attempt to reach for my purse.

In a couple of elegant moves, Sienna steps into my way and takes it from me.

"No, you're not going to run. We need to talk."

"No, you should have told me who you were right away. There's nothing to talk about. Now get out of my way!"

"Please."

"No. Leave me alone. You have to let me go—"

"Courtney! Listen to me! I didn't kill Tommy, and neither did anyone in my family!"

She holds my hands, then embraces me tightly, and I wish I was that badass and pushed her back, but instead I melt into her embrace, let go, let it all out the way I never have before. It's irrational and stupid, but for a moment, I feel safe to do so.

"It's okay," she whispers, holding me, brushing her hand over my hair as I cry on her shoulder, a big ugly embarrassing cry, over everything I've lost. Including the trust I put in her, the fleeting hope that we could be more than a torrid affair while I figure out my life.

Courtney Flynn. Sienna Caruso. Impossible.

Eventually, embarrassment takes over, and I slowly, reluctantly disentangle myself.

"I need to...in there." I point to the bathroom.

"You won't try to squeeze through the window? It's pretty high up. I don't want you to hurt yourself."

"You planned all of it so I couldn't get away, didn't you?"

She doesn't deny it. "You are safe here too," she insists.

I don't know that a safe place exists for me, anywhere, but I really do need to wash my face.

A part of me still wishes I could believe her.

"I'm aware I owe you an explanation," she says when we sit down by the window, with the promised river view. I still feel raw, but my priorities are back in place.

"You weren't lying to me? About Oliver being safe?"

"He and Jade are, I swear."

Perhaps I shouldn't be so easily reassured, but it is a relief.

"I'm not surprised you found out. I knew you would eventually, with that cover coming out."

"Why didn't you just tell me then?" I'm frustrated with her, but mostly with me, because the memory of her touch lingers, and it's not all about consolation. How can I still be attracted to her after she lied to me? But I am, and a part of me regrets that she's not likely to want me after this. I'm a mess. This was a huge mistake, but I can't turn away now, not when she might be able to give me some of the answers I've been chasing.

"When I saw you in the lobby, I had no idea why you came to town, whether you were there on an errand for your in-laws."

I can't help it, I snort at her reasoning. "Yeah, right. Given everything I've told you when I really shouldn't have, you should be able to tell they wouldn't trust me with errands, let

71

alone something more important. I've never had anything to do with the business, ever."

"Your choice? Or Tommy's?"

"You know the answer to that too. Wait a minute, why are you interrogating me?"

"No one's interrogating anyone," she assures me. "I had to check up on a few things, and eventually, I realized you weren't here on Rory and Ciara's behalf. I'm afraid the moment was never right. But we're here now, and we might as well have that conversation. They are mistaken, and they have been for a long time. They never took responsibility for that botched delivery, and it nearly destroyed our reputation. No, we weren't thrilled about that, but we didn't plan to murder Tommy in return."

"They say he was with your cousin Nico that night. That he followed Tommy out in the alley and shot him."

Even as I say it, it becomes clear to me that I've lived with bits and pieces of what might be wild conspiracy theories. I wouldn't put that past Rory. If they aren't, then I'm far from home in a hotel room with a member of a family who hates the Flynns.

"That's not what happened," Sienna objects. "They met, spent some time together in the bar. Tommy went outside for a smoke, when he didn't return, Nico went to check on him. That's when the shooting happened."

"What about the witness? Wasn't he a cop?"

"I don't know why he said what he said, but your in-laws haven't told you the whole story. The testimony was later disputed. It was dark, things happened fast."

"Also, the main suspect was never apprehended," I say matter-of-factly.

"No, because he didn't do it. Courtney. This crazy argument has to stop. We didn't kill anyone. We had good business relations once, and they destroyed it by selling us a bad product and not owning up to it. That is what happened. If someone came after Tommy over some botched drug deal, it wasn't one of us."

"Drug deal?" My voice goes up a few notches, to the region of shrill. "He would have never…No. They import whiskey from their own distillery, for Christ's sake."

Her gaze on me is sympathetic, and I want to yell at her again, but the truth is, there's nothing I know for sure.

"Which is what I could use right now."

"I can get you something to drink in a minute. Look, I don't have all the insights of their business. All I know is that they've been accusing us ever since, and it's simply a lie. Those were some fine whiskeys. It would have been in the interest of both families to properly investigate the incident and move on from it. Rory didn't want to. So, here we are."

To say I feel naïve would be the understatement of the year.

"Is there any way we could prove it?"

"I don't know. Maybe. It wouldn't be easy after all these years. Stopping with the wild accusations would help. I'm sorry I didn't tell you. But I had to protect my own family first."

Her family, Tommy's.

"Now what?"

"I understand you've been between a rock and a hard place, but if you want to find out more, I'll help you."

"Why?"

She holds my gaze as she says, "Because I don't want you to go, Courtney. And I am sorry too."

I am still too easy. Curious. Hungry. I nod, aware that I, once again, put everything on the line. It will be worth it, because one day, Oliver will ask the hard questions. I'll be able to give him the answers he deserves.

That, and it's hard to pretend I don't want to stay.

Chapter Twelve

Sienna

I'm aware I'm still on thin ice, but perhaps it's better this way, raise all these subjects here rather than close to home—because they are way too close to home.

I'm getting a clearer picture though, maybe more so than I have from the reports I definitely won't tell her about. She knows I had to look into her, and we leave it at that.

I look at her, sitting across from me, still wondering, and I feel for her a whole lot more than I ever thought I would for a Flynn. Because she isn't. In name only. That doesn't mean she doesn't harbor a lot of feelings for her late husband, ranging from love to anger to deep bone-cutting grief.

Feelings are complicated. For her. For me. There was a reason why I didn't date, but refrained to quick, meaningless interactions every now and then. I hired an escort service once, all with the goal to avoid messy relations or let anyone get too close.

It's too late for that now. It's messy already, and Courtney has gotten under my skin.

I must live with the consequences.

"I'll help you," I say again. "I can find out who that cop was." I have a vague idea, but I don't want to share with her until I know more. She has enough on her mind as it is.

"That would be a start," she agrees. "And...thank you." With a rueful smile, she adds, "I can't believe I lost it so completely."

"You had to hold it together for a long time. And you didn't know who you could trust." I don't mean to sneakily vilify Rory and Ciara. They are by no means innocent.

"I really don't want them to do with Oliver what they did with Tommy, setting him on such a narrow path when he's still a child. He might have a knack for business, or not. I want that to be his choice."

Yes, she might still be a bit naïve. But if she can get away from their influence and the way they make their money, her plan just might work.

"You're his mom. Where he lives and goes to school is your decision."

This time, her smile is void of all the conflicted emotions between us, and simply grateful.

"Can you believe that this is the first time someone has said it out loud?"

"It's the truth. Now, this has been deep. How about we continue over dinner?"

"I'd like that."

"Good. I promised to let you look at the menu, so..." I pick up the leather-bound folder and hand it to her. "Anything you want. This is the all-inclusive option, and even if it wasn't..."

"You're the boss," she comments, a trace of amusement to her tone now.

"I am indeed. I was planning to spoil you so go ahead."

Despite the offer, her choices are almost modest, which, I guess, goes with the unexpectedly sober turn this getaway has taken.

Nevertheless, food and drinks are of the highest quality, and it helps with the subject matter.

"Is there anything you remember from that time, anything that might help?" I ask.

"The police asked me that, and I went over it so many times in my head. I was in shock. I didn't know what to think, especially when they suggested Tommy might be involved in any criminal activities. Not drugs, they didn't say that, but now I wonder if they left out that part."

"Not necessarily. If Tommy kept a clean house, the random attack is still on the table I suppose. But without irrefutable proof, Rory and Ciara will never believe it."

"It can't be easy, being always at war like that," she says thoughtfully. "Is it really so foolish to think that it could ever change?"

Perhaps it is, but we're not there yet.

"The rumors they spread caused us a lot of loss of revenue. You can imagine we were not happy with that, but perhaps there's a way we could go back to the table."

Courtney shakes her head. "I've been tapdancing around the subject for such a long time. I don't want to do that anymore. I want the truth."

"So do I."

"Then why don't we start with your cousin Nico?" The question is quite spirited.

"We all talked to him, me, my uncle, my aunt...He isn't a murderer. He didn't even carry that night. I believe him, and we couldn't take the chance that Rory might have someone in the police."

"Get out," is her answer, her disbelief audible. "So, you're saying you know that something illegal was going on? Look, I don't want to do the tapdancing with you too. Are they or aren't they involved in something? I remember some men coming by, and I don't think they were Tommy's friends. They looked like...militia or something." She cringes, and I can imagine. It's a long way from a vacation romance to being a wife and mother in a mob family. We don't think of ourselves as better than them, but there are some lines that the Flynns have crossed. As long as they weren't crossing into our territory and business, fine, but it didn't stop there. Unfortunately.

"I don't think you'd like the answer, and do you really need to know as long as being Oliver's grandparents is all they are to you? Look, Courtney, I have a family and a business to protect too. I like you, and the reason why I invited you here regardless of who you were married to is that you're still outside of it all."

"Outside." She laughs bitterly. "That's a good way to describe it."

"Believe me, it's better that way. Truth be told the chances that Rory would come to the table are slim, even if we could come up with proof—which we will try to do, anyway. He's invested in the story now."

"But why?"

If I told her about territories and profits and overlapping interests, it might freak her out. Then again, she's almost there.

"Those men who came to the house, could you find out names? Were they close to Rory? Someone might have wanted a bigger piece than they were owed."

She groans, then takes a sip of her wine before she sets the glass down and covers her face with her hands. "This is a nightmare. Why didn't I wake up earlier? Do something?"

"You're too hard on yourself. What are you to do when your husband asks you to live with him in a castle?"

"Never worked out too well for the princesses in fairy tales," she returns. "Oh God, Sienna, what am I going to do?"

"Exactly what you planned. Go meet your former classmate on Sunday, get you and Oliver settled. When the time is right, talk to your in-laws. Every once in a while, go on a date with me. I wasn't joking, by the way. I am interested in trying the cake Oliver and Jade are making."

Courtney is laughing anyway.

"You are right. It's much too early to determine what he should do or wants to do. Maybe he's going to become a world-famous pastry chef."

She's still laughing, and then stops abruptly. "I thought I had it all figured out," she says. "I think I am losing my mind."

Her eyes seek mine, and I take my time to understand what I'm seeing, beyond what I want to see, the yearning in her tone.

I get to my feet, and at the same time, she does the same. I reach out and pull her to me. No one's going to pretend or sugarcoat anything any longer. There are few guarantees in life, but I did promise her something, and I still plan on delivering. When I kiss her, she clings to me, hands eagerly pulling my blouse out of my skirt, eager to touch skin. I gasp when they do.

This could have gone wrong in so many ways, and frankly, it still might once she pulls away more layers of the truth.

However, I didn't lie about Tommy, or Nico. And as long as she doesn't plan to go home to Rory and Ciara, there won't be any problem.

Just this, the perfect bliss born out of a twist of fate. I pull her with me to the bedroom, but instead of moving to the bed, I choose one of the armchairs, and she's straddling my lap. I run my hands up her thighs, underneath her dress, drawing my fingers over the fabric of her panties until she moans. Finally, I touch her, satisfied with the course of my mission as proof of her arousal coats my fingertips, warm and wet.

Her body welcomes me, the pleasure I'm going to grant her, but still, she leans forward to bury her face against my neck. It only takes a few minutes for her to tumble over the brink, and when she does, I nearly go along with her. I hold on to her as she stiffens, then slumps into my arms.

"We'll figure it out," I promise her.

And even if we don't, we still have a few hours ahead of us. That, I don't have to say out loud.

After a few moments of catching her breath, she slides to the floor, kneeling between my thighs as she gently opens them. As Courtney looks up at me, I know that we were right to take a chance. She has seen too much, been given too much pressure by the Flynns not to understand what's going on, and I know I can trust her.

There's no going back for either of us.

Chapter Thirteen

Courtney

My mind is still reeling from all the revelations, while a part of me is relieved they've been made. Given all the shadows and lies that surround us, I find it hard to be angry at Sienna much longer. I don't know that I would have thought my arrival in town, just as she was trying to restore the family business's former reputation, was a coincidence.

She doesn't say it out loud, but I sense that she's just as tired of all the machinations. Racketeering, drugs, guns, all those subjects the police asked me about when I was near hysterical with grief, she doesn't want anything to do with it either.

And maybe she's right, we can help each other.

I think we already are.

Later that night, she orders champagne with dessert, and we retreat to the bed for the occasion. I have often felt exhausted in the past few years. This is a different kind, the one that makes you feel at home in your body.

I'm no longer beside myself.

Whatever stories Rory has told, has perhaps been fed, about the Carusos, aren't true, and if we're lucky, we'll be able to prove it. Then we'd both be free, and I could raise Oliver the way I see fit.

I smile to myself thinking about introducing Sienna to him, then getting mad at her when she went ahead. What a wild day this has been. If this works out, we'll all get closure, and what could be wrong with that?

I fall asleep remembering when I told Tommy about Diana Wynter, shortly after we got engaged. It was never a problem for him, he never questioned my identity. I'd like to think that if we can lay this feud to rest, he might want me to try.

I'm still wrestling with the idea of what he was, what this family still is—but I'm no longer alone trying to find those answers.

I slip into a dream with her naked body wrapped around me, wake up alone and spend a few terrified seconds until I find the note.

Went for a swim. Come join me when you wake up.

Not likely, I think, my heart beating faster again when I think of the water, the deep end, the smell of chlorine. It's not that I don't want to. I just can't. Not all questions need answers.

I check on Jade and Oliver next.

We just had blueberry pancakes, she texts. *Olli says hi, and that we kept a piece of cake for the pretty lady.*

I get out of bed and into the shower, body memories of last night's activities lingering pleasantly. I need all the pleasure I can get to make it through the next few days.

Lucky me, Sienna returns at that moment. She walks inside the bathroom, taking off her robe and then the red bikini she's wearing underneath.

I just stand there and look at her, the amusement in her expression showing me that she's reading me like a book.

"I thought I might take my shower upstairs," she says after opening the door of the stall. "You didn't want to come to the pool?"

"No," I answer and pull her inside under the rainforest shower.

Not all questions need answers, but I need the magic her hands and lips do on my body just one more time.

Sienna has no objections.

—ee—

The ride home is quiet, both of us hanging on to our own thoughts. We'll meet again, strategize before I talk to Rory and Ciara, but we're both aware that there's a lot on the line. For the two of us, for people we care about. When the driver parks in front of Jade's apartment building, she takes my hand and squeezes it gently, silent reassurance.

I can't believe I yelled at her. That I believed she might be involved in Tommy's murder. It's about time I formed my own opinions again. It will be challenging, no doubt.

Sienna walks me up to the apartment where Oliver greets us enthusiastically. She gives me a surprised smile when he hugs her too, albeit a bit shy and reluctant.

The pretty lady will be around. I hope he's going to be all right with that.

"That is so kind of you," Sienna says when Jade hands her the box with the cake.

"We promised, right, Olli? It's pretty good if I may say so."

"I have no doubts. You have a good day. Courtney, I'll call you."

Then she's gone, and I have to take a moment to reorient myself.

"She's nice. A bit crazy," Jade says. "She wouldn't take no for an answer, but you can tell her I don't need all that money just to babysit for a few hours. Put it in a college fund for Oliver."

She doesn't know half of the story, and I have too little time for it now. I do want to come clean with her. It matters to me. It will have to wait until Sienna and I have more proof of the real chain of events.

She knows how to handle herself in this context, has a lot more experience with it than I do. I don't want to involve Jade unless I know for sure it's safe.

"I take it you're not going to share any details," she says mildly. "I had some hope of living vicariously."

"Please. Don't," I say, and she laughs.

"I was kidding. I think she's good for you. That's all that matters."

I wish that was the truth, but for the moment, it is.

We stay a bit longer but head back to the hotel before dinner, considering that tomorrow, we're going to check into the inn. On the way to our room, we walk past the pool, reminding me of this morning. Someone opens the door, and I catch a whiff of the tell-tale smells, hastening my step.

"Mommy, when are we going home?" Oliver asks, and before I can give him an answer, a voice behind us speaks, "We were wondering that ourselves."

I'm startled enough for the key card to slip from my fingers. I pick it up and turn to Rory. To my relief, he doesn't seem angry, even gives me a smile before he crouches down to greet Oliver.

"Grandpa! We had a great time with Jade! I made a cake yesterday!"

"Is that so? It sounds nice."

"It's very good. Would you like a piece?"

"Later, maybe," Rory says, and I tense as his tone changes slightly. "First, I need to talk to your mom for a bit. Courtney? Can we do this in private?"

"I just came back—" I bite my lip, unwilling to share that Oliver spent the night at Jade's, and I...No. I'm not sure I'd like to invite him to my room either, under the circumstances. "Could you wait for me in the lobby? We'll get a couple of toys for Oliver, and then we can sit and have a coffee." Not that I need more caffeine. I have no idea what I'm doing.

He let me stay at the mansion when I lost everything, made sure my son and I were taken care of. I'm grateful for that. But he also wants Oliver to carry a dangerous torch, and I'm not okay with that.

"I think I'll wait here," he says, gesturing to the hallway. "You won't be long, right?"

Did he think I was going to run—again? Did it cross my mind, yes. But I want to keep things as normal as possible as long as my child is around.

In the room, Oliver picks his coloring book, some pencils, and a stuffed toy, and we join Rory again.

"You had some business to take care of in town?" I ask.

"No. We had a few questions." He lowers his voice as he continues. "And I don't know that you want Oliver to be present for this."

"I could call Jade and see if..."

"No, don't do that," he says with a sigh. "We'll make it work."

In the lobby café, we find a semi-private table and order coffee. I get a muffin for Oliver which gets me a raised eyebrow. Yes, we just brought cake home, but if this conversation is turning serious, I want him to be distracted from it. I briefly wonder about the babysitter service Sienna mentioned, but it's probably on too short notice. Besides, I feel better having eyes on him.

Oliver shows Rory his princess coloring book, and much to his credit, he praises his coloring skills rather than comment on the content.

When he turns to me, the smile is gone.

"Truth be told, we would have never expected this of you, and I have to tell you we are extremely disappointed."

"What? Why?"

My mind is racing. I had considered that they might keep tabs on me, but do they really already know about the job? About...

"I'm sorry I haven't been answering Ciara's messages. I've been...busy."

"With the woman who killed our son, your husband?"

Okay, so that's what it's all about. They do know.

"Sienna Caruso didn't kill Tommy. She and her family had no interest in doing so."

The gloves are finally off. It's a bizarre setting, speaking difficult truths in polite tones so the one person we both care about doesn't notice.

"And you know that how?" He shakes his head. "It would be best for all of us if you came back home with me, and we forgot about it. That's the best we can offer you at this point. We haven't changed our minds regarding Oliver, and we'll still help you with his school."

"Rory. I'm sorry, but I'm not coming home. I have a job and a place to live lined up. You've done so much for us, and I'm beyond grateful, but I can't depend on your generosity forever."

"Maybe," he's quick to acknowledge. "But Tommy cared about you, and that means something to us. Besides, it's about Oliver's future more than anything. We can offer him everything he deserves."

What if he doesn't want what you're offering him? It's on the tip of my tongue to ask this question. Back home I was preoccupied, sometimes intimidated, but it's not the same anymore.

I'm not the same.

"I'm his mother."

"I thought this was going to be challenging for both of us," Rory acknowledges. "That's exactly the reason why I didn't want Oliver to be around for this conversation, and I think I found the best possible solution. I know a place where we can have dinner and figure all of this out in private."

"Hi, Courtney."

I jump to my feet at the sound of her voice. Saoirse. What is she doing here?

"If you give me the key card, I can take Oliver up to his room, and, if necessary, put him to bed later. Bedtime story included." She winks at him, and he smiles.

I am dumbfounded. And mad.

"No way. You can't do this. You can't take him..." I realize that he's watching attentively now, and lower my voice. "This isn't going to work. Oliver and I will stay here."

"The last word's not been spoken on that yet," Rory returns. "Would you please calm down? I just want to talk in private tonight, that's all. I'm going to take you to dinner, and Saoirse will watch my grandson." I don't think the emphasis on the relation is random. I am the opposite of calm. What if I called Sienna? She promised to help.

"Tommy trusted Saoirse with his life," he says impatiently. "She will take good care of Oliver."

"He better be here when I come back."

"He and I will be in your room when you return." Saoirse's tone is laced with indulgence. "Don't worry. And if I were you, I wouldn't want to miss the opportunity. Rory knows the best places in town."

Outsider. Sienna thought it was a good thing, but I'm not so sure. They don't miss any occasion to let me know. Between the three of us, there's a lot of knowledge I've never asked for. It's true that Tommy put a lot of trust in Saoirse. She might have been more to him than a trusted bodyguard.

This is all wrong, but I don't see much of a choice. They won't harm my child. They just don't care that much about me. I'll have to figure out a way to make both work in my favor. Even though Sienna said it's too early, maybe the tentative alliance we formed can help convince Rory that I'm not the traitor he might think I am.

"I cared about Tommy, too, you know. And I know you mean well, but you can't keep doing this, blindsiding me like this."

"Are we going to have dinner? We had an early lunch." To Saoirse he says, "Order anything you want, and I'll clear the bill when we leave tomorrow."

He still thinks that Oliver and I are going with him. Maybe it's not so bad to have some uninterrupted time, because I can't make a mistake here. I need to make him see that it's not going to happen.

As Saoirse walks away with my son, holding his hand, I watch them with a mix of resentment and unease. I've always been uneasy about her, her beauty and confidence. Looks like she's charmed Oliver too—he is his father's son after all, noticing a "pretty lady" when he sees one.

Before my thoughts can get any weirder, I wrench them back to the present. I have my work cut out for me.

———eee———

Rory takes me to a pub downtown, where the owner and a few patrons greet him like an old friend, and I know that wasn't a coincidence. He introduces me as "Tommy's wife" and tells them we're in town for business.

"Jack is a good friend of mine," he says when we sit down at a table.

"That's...nice."

"You've been around us long enough to know we take care of our friends, and our family."

"I have," I acknowledge. "And like I said, I appreciate everything. I couldn't have done it alone after...Tommy."

"But that's the point, you didn't have to. And now you're ready to throw it all away for your fling with that woman?"

I nearly choke on the beer he's ordered.

"Courtney," he says patiently, "did you think we wouldn't find out?"

"It's not what you think," I hurry to explain. "Sienna would like to have everyone back at the table, find out what really happened to Tommy that night. Her family is not responsible."

"She says that?" He laughs bitterly. "And you believe her over us? Got you wrapped around her little finger quickly. Bitch is lying whenever she opens her mouth. Excuse my language, but these are the people who murdered my son."

"I'm sorry. I used to think...It wasn't them, Rory. I'm pretty sure."

He shakes his head in frustration. "I don't think you understand. Look, we are aware, it's been years. All you've done is take care of Oliver, which is commendable, but I'm sure you were lonely. Tommy wouldn't have wanted you to grieve for the rest of your life. It's not that she's a woman. We imagined that might happen, Tommy told us. It's that she's a Caruso. They shipped the killer over to Europe, and he's been evading the authorities ever since."

"Well, he's not the only one, I guess."

His eyes narrow. "What's that supposed to mean?"

"The men who came to the house sometimes? Do you trust them? Did Tommy? Something went terribly wrong that night, but it wasn't Nico Caruso's fault. They were friends!"

"God, Courtney, you're naïve." Rory rarely raises his voice, and he doesn't have to.

The accusation brings heat to my face. All of it, the complete dismissal of everything I've said, the fact that Tommy shared something this intimate with his parents. Saoirse, back at the hotel with my son. I want to cry, but that would only further their impression of me as weak, easily influenceable.

I am not. I know Sienna told me the truth, because I understood what she was saying between the lines. That Tommy wasn't somebody innocent, that she isn't. But they didn't murder him.

"I am realistic. Her family had a lot to lose, and nothing to gain from Tommy's death."

"Did you even pay attention?" he asks. "They accused us of poisoning their guests with a bad product. It was all a lie. And when they couldn't get away with it, they killed Tommy. Was that always the plan? Who knows, but it was Nico Caruso who followed him into that alley and shot him."

I can see the pain in his expression, and it evokes an echo within me, the memory of that night when I had to listen to the horrific news with a baby on my arm, my son who would never see his father again.

"What if there was someone else?"

"Well, there was. A witness who saw Nico run away. Before he boarded a plane straight to Naples."

"Okay. Wait a second. Wasn't that statement disputed?"

He picks up his phone and shows me a picture of a man in uniform, mid-fifties.

"Look at this man. He's a highly decorated officer, put his life on the line to serve his community for decades. You really think he made that up?"

Do I? My mind is in chaos. I remember him now. He, too, came to the house sometimes, meeting with Rory and Tommy in his office.

That doesn't mean anything, just that he might have been under duress, mistaken, simply too far away in the dark to identify the shooter.

What if it was Nico Caruso? It's probably as hard for Sienna to believe as it is to imagine Rory as some kind of mob boss. And yet...

I wish that we could just go somewhere far away from it all, Oliver, Sienna and me.

"You need to come home, Courtney," he concludes. "That's the only way. We have an obligation to family, and our legacy, and you're one of us."

It occurs to me that it's the first time he's said that.

Flattery? Pressure?

"Like Saoirse." Two can play that game.

"Stop being childish. You and I know if Saoirse had been with him, Tommy would still be alive."

Another statement never made openly, and it makes the color drain from my face. He doesn't mean just that night. He's saying what was on their mind all this time, that she would have been the better, the preferred wife.

I've heard everything I needed to hear.

"Thank you for dinner," I say. "Please, take me back to my son now. And when you go home tomorrow, give Ciara my best. Oliver and I are staying, and I'm starting my new job on Monday."

Chapter Fourteen

Sienna

I'm back in my office early, contemplating the past few days. The sheer rush of it, the recklessness, the pleasure. Sipping my first coffee of the day, I indulge myself, reveling in the memory.

Though, you can't deny there's a pragmatic side to it. The kind of campaign that the Flynns have been waging cost resources, it's been detrimental for both sides. It would help a great deal if we could all be adults. We don't have to be friends.

I realize I might have gotten ahead of myself when Aunt Simona calls my office number.

"Sienna, where are you? Francesco and I have been trying to get a hold of you."

"Simona, what happened?" The woman is pretty much unshakeable, so to hear the barely suppressed alarm and anger in her voice is a concern. That's when I realize I haven't even turned on my cell phone yet. A hazardous omission. It's blazing with multiple messages.

"Someone vandalized one of the Grand Palace Resorts. They drove a car into the lobby and sprayed the walls. Matteo almost caught one of them, but he got hurt."

"What? How is he?" I'm out of my chair, any thought of recent pleasures far from my mind now.

"In the hospital with a concussion and broken ribs. Doctors say he's going to be okay, and none of the guests got hurt, but Sienna, it's a mess, just when things were calming down! This is going to cost us!"

I compose myself in a heartbeat. "I'll come over right away. What do we know? About this? Gang-related? Some teens on drugs?"

"Think, Sienna," she says bitterly. "We all know who's behind this."

"What do you mean?"

Uncle Francesco is on the line a second later.

"Sienna, please. Rory Flynn is in town, along with his daughter-in-law. What do you think that means? They saw we have a leg up, and they don't like it. As usual, they resort to mob tactics."

"Wait! Francesco. Courtney isn't on best terms with her in-laws. There's no way she's in on this, if it wasn't just a co-incidence."

"Be careful what you say," he says. "They met at her hotel yesterday, then had dinner at the Shamrock. Looks like they get along pretty well to me."

"No." I shake my head even though he can't see me. "I don't know about Rory, but Courtney wants to get away from it all. I spoke to her. She understands—and she might be the only one—that we didn't kill Tommy Flynn. In fact, she and I were going to look into it."

There's silence on the other end, before Francesco speaks.

"We'll talk about this another time. For now, it's important that you stay objective. Whatever she says, she's still Tommy's widow."

And she's her own woman, too, I think, but it's not the time to get into it with him. There are steps we need to take.

"I'll swing by the hospital, and then I'll join you. You already contacted the insurance?"

"Of course. Get here as soon as you can."

So much for being adults. I curse before I pick up my coat and purse, leaving my coffee and a few illusions behind.

Even if Rory wasn't involved, any notion of peace, or even a ceasefire, has become that much more distant.

My cousin Matteo is miserable and pissed, but at least he'll be okay. That's a relief. I ask a few questions, but he doesn't remember much. There were two of them. They wore masks, of course, and the one who sprayed the walls, hit Matteo in the head before he got back in the truck, and they fled.

"Francesco tells me that Rory Flynn is in the area," he says grimly. "They've cost us enough. It's time to do something for good."

"Let's not jump to conclusions. I hear Rory Flynn came to visit his grandson."

It's all chaos in my head, and I hate it. I barely can remember a time when the Flynn's weren't enemies. Clearly, they're not innocent. But they have already drawn a connection to Courtney, and I don't want her or Oliver in the line of fire. Or Jade Summers. I'll have to give them a heads-up.

Matteo gives me an incredulous frown.

"Look at this!" he says, pointing to the bandage on his arm. "Could have been worse, but almost the entire building is down, and you want to play semantics? Of course, the old man goes to see his grandson before he causes havoc. Probably is training him as we speak."

"Oliver Flynn is four years old!" I can't help raising my voice. Courtney is right. It's ridiculous to start coaching her young son for any position in the family business. I started young, but even I was allowed to have a childhood. He's just a little boy.

"And you might want to check if your priorities are still in the right place," he shoots back, and winces. "Damn it, Sienna. You've been seen around town with Courtney. Whatever that's about, and I honestly don't want to know, people are bound to talk."

I stiffen at this tone. "What are you saying?"

"I don't have to spell it out to you, do I?"

"You're questioning my loyalty? I've taken this business to where it is now." No point in starting an argument with him either, but I've just about had it. "I work around the clock, and the moment I take twenty-four hours, people think I'm abandoning ship?"

"Don't deflect. It's not about taking a vacation, it's about who you've been with. Now I know you've been pouring everything you've got into the hotel business."

"So you and everyone else could do what you're doing on the side."

"Beside the point. Whatever you have to do, be careful. She's one of them."

On his last sentence, the nurse appears, probably about to kick me out.

"That's all right. I'll go. I'll be back, Matteo, and I hope you find some common sense until then. Let's just wait until we have the official report? Those might have been kids from the neighborhood, drunk and high on something."

"Yeah, right," he scoffs, and I leave.

When I'm in my car, I see that I have a couple of messages from Courtney.

There's no time, I decide. I'll take care of my family first—even if they irritate me to no end—and then I'll call her back, see if she picked up anything from Rory.

I also want to know what he's been doing in town. Even if he didn't hire anyone to vandalize one of our resorts, if he came to harass Courtney and Oliver, I'll put an end to that too.

I might be the face of the legitimate business, but I have enough people that answer to me to keep her safe.

The site of the incident is indeed sobering, broken glass everywhere, police, nervous hotel staff trying to calm guests. I overhear a few of them asking to check out. I'll make sure they get a voucher, so hopefully the reviews won't be too bad. I can't deny the damage is done. To the property, once more, our reputation, and likely, to any attempt at a peace deal.

The timing is bad, given that we're in the middle of a big push for expansion. The insurance will pay since there is no fault on our side, but until then, we're bleeding money.

When I get to talk to Francesco and Simona in an office on the other side of the resort, the tears in her eyes make me furious. They are right, whoever did this, is going to pay. I want them in prison, I want to sue them, or the ones who hired them, for every last cent.

It's clear that my aunt and uncle are not thinking among the same lines.

"Whatever you do, don't do anything rash," I warn them. "We need to wait for the report."

"What's there to wait for?" he asks, incredulously. "They've been running around accusing us of damaging their reputation, when they are the ones who delivered a bad product and nearly got a couple of our guests killed."

I know the story. I've heard it a million times.

"History repeats itself. And, you didn't forget that Nico couldn't come home in years because they keep lying about him and Tommy Flynn. No, I don't think we have to wait. I'm tired of all the waiting, and frankly, Sienna, you should be too."

"What are you going to do?"

"We," he corrects. "It's about time that we worked on this together. You did a great job with the Morettis. Now we have to do it again."

For a few seconds, I'm in the unusual position of being speechless. And beyond apprehensive, because that was an entirely different story. Joey Moretti and his clan were a pain. Everyone's pain. When the opportunity presented itself, I stepped in, a little push here, a little machination there, and our friends the Falcones did the rest. Okay. Friends. They're friendly, and so I've never had a problem letting them think ending the Morettis was all their doing.

This, it's different. It's personal, and the stakes are so much higher...and not just because it's Courtney calling me right now.

"Excuse me," I say. "I have to take this."

I step outside the door, start talking right away after I answer. "I'm sorry, but I don't have a lot of time this morning. Can I call you later?"

"Sienna. I'm freaking out. I'm so scared they're going to take Oliver away from me."

"What? Who?" I ask even though I already know. The pain in her voice cuts deep, and I nearly curse once more, or that BS we have to deal with because of the egos of men who came before us. I'm so tired of it.

"Rory. And Saoirse." She takes a deep breath. "I'm sorry. I don't mean to bother you, and I sure as hell don't mean to sound so hysterical, but they want me to come back."

Saoirse Reilly, Flynn's bodyguard, and perhaps more. Flynn brought backup. If anyone of them is to blame for the incident, it's certainly not Courtney, and she might be in danger from the same people that attacked us.

There must be some accountability.

"I'm sorry," she says with a sigh. "I just...I was hoping we could talk."

"No, that's okay. I need to talk to you too. Can you meet me in an hour? Until then, don't answer the door, to anyone."

"Rory said they will be back."

"I don't care what he says." I have to make a call and let my investigator know that our focus is shifting from Courtney to her father-in-law. One hour is not nearly enough for everything I need to do, but I need to see her, and I have to get back to the office to check on that information I got about that cop witness on the night of Tommy's murder. "Look, I could..." Make another call. Send a couple of our own people.

Then again, I've never been good at delegating, and it's worked fine for me so far. "Forget what I said. I'm coming right over. Don't let anyone in until I'm there. I mean it."

"Okay. Thank you."

"It's no problem." It might be the first outright lie I've told her. It's going to be a major problem, but I want her to be safe.

Chapter Fifteen

Courtney

Maybe Sienna is the last person I should involve in this when as of now, I only have her word and my helpless infatuation for the woman. Then again, I don't know who else to call, to trust. My parents, who live on the other side of the country, can't do anything about this situation. I vowed not to involve Jade in anything dangerous. Will might reconsider giving me a job if he knows the whole truth. He already graciously agreed to postpone for a day.

I'm running out of options. Silly of me to think they could let me start over here with Oliver. But realistically, what can they do?

I can't think straight. I've been up all night, unable to sleep, watching Oliver as if someone was going to sneak into the room and take him from me.

Rory made it very clear that he wants to take both of us home. That's what he says, anyway. I know he wants Oliver above all, and he's aware that I'm not going to leave him, at least not freely.

Sienna isn't likely going to change all of it, but I'm already feeling calmer after hearing her voice. Another point of view, someone telling me that I'm not going to lose, not again.

I am far past wondering if Rory and Ciara are, if Tommy might have been involved in something illegal. I'm not ruling out going to the police, though I'd hardly know what to tell them. I tried to run. It didn't work. Now I have to fight, and Sienna is the best ally I can think of. Also, I need to see her again.

Sienna knocks on my door exactly seventeen minutes after we've hung up, and she brings two large coffees and a bag of pastries.

"You're a lifesaver!" I jump to my feet and kiss her, since Oliver is only just starting to stir. "I didn't dare call room service."

"Good choice. When I said no one, I meant no one."

She returns the kiss, but only briefly. Her demeanor is beyond serious, and I'm beginning to understand that it's not just because of my own situation.

Sienna puts down breakfast on the coffee table after she has assured herself that the door is locked properly. She even gazes outside the window, but we're on the tenth floor. I don't think there could be danger from outside...I can't think about this now.

"Courtney, we need to talk. There's been an incident at one of our resorts. Someone drove a car into the lobby, spray-painted on the walls."

My hand goes to my mouth.

"Was anybody hurt?"

"Nothing too serious. We were lucky, this time, but it's a damn mess. Courtney, did Rory mention anything..."

"No." The first sip of coffee sits heavy in my stomach now. "He didn't say anything to me about vandalizing your hotels, and I can't believe you came here to ask me that."

"Courtney. Please." A bit of that ice vanishes from her voice, and the woman I thought I knew, was getting to know, is back. "I didn't come to accuse you of anything. I am worried about you. Rory showing up at this moment, and whatever his intentions regarding Oliver are..." Much to her credit, she lowers her voice. Oliver has turned over and fallen asleep again.

I press my hand against my forehead, as if I could ward off all those terrible thoughts. No such luck. And whichever way you put it, we are in the middle of this.

"I'm sorry about what happened, but I swear, I have no idea who did it, or if Rory had anything to do with it. Don't you think you'd be the first one I'd tell? He showed up here yesterday with Saoirse and gave me a lecture about honor and loyalty, how I owe the family. I asked Will if I could start a day later. He said yes, but I can't stall him forever. Rory insists that Oliver and I come home. I don't know what to do."

"They can't make you," Sienna states. "Look, you were going to work at reception. If that falls through, you could come work for us."

I can't help it, I start laughing, even though I feel more like crying.

"What's funny about this?"

"It's not. I'm sorry." It's absurd, that's what it is, me running away, or trying to, because of my late husband's family's shady business, straight to the Carusos who, in Rory's opinion, are the worst. Murderers. "Nothing funny about any of it. What are we going to do? I swear I don't know what exactly Rory and Saoirse are up to except bringing Oliver back home, but I know he's not looking to make peace. He scolded me for being seen with you."

"Word gets around," Sienna says calmly. "Does it bother you?"

"I want to start my new job. Make a life with Oliver. I don't care what they think." I don't want to, anyway. "They've kept things from me. Tommy did, obviously. I just don't want Oliver around all this."

"I understand. I've had someone look into that cop."

"Oh." I had forgotten about that for a moment. I think about the timing of all of this. "Hollis, right? I asked Rory about him, and he slapped a picture on the table and told me that I was not to question this man's integrity."

"Dinner must have been fun," Sienna mumbles. I ignore that she obviously already knows about it.

"Anyway, I remembered that he met with Tommy sometimes. I don't know what they discussed, or if it was anything shady..." She can't hide her amusement at my choice of words. "But it adds up, doesn't it?"

"That it does. What about Saoirse?"

"Does she have it in her to pull off something like that?" That, too, seems absurd to me. "To be honest? I doubt it. I mean she's been around as long as I can remember, and she's definitely loyal." I recall her tears at Tommy's funeral. They spoke volumes when I was wrapped so tightly in a cocoon of shock that this kind of display of emotion felt impossible. Saoirse didn't hold back.

"Maybe, but that wasn't what I meant. We have three people confirmed at or near the scene that night. Tommy. Nico who didn't do it. Hollis. What if there was someone else?"

"You're thinking...?" An icy hand clamps itself around my heart when I think of her being alone with Oliver last night.

Sienna takes a sip. She looks pensive. "I'm not saying it's what happened, but we're looking for someone who had insight in this ongoing fight between our families. Someone for whom it would be convenient to blame Nico."

"I don't know if I can do this. Now, I mean. I'm grateful that you want to help me, but..."

"I understand. You have a lot going on right now." She lays a hand on my shoulder, comforting me. If it wasn't for my son right here in the room, I might seek a different kind of comfort. I am so tired.

"Look who's talking. Unfortunately, you are right." Sienna sighs before she takes a bite of her pastry, savoring it as if stalling.

No one can relate more than me.

"You need to go back?"

"In a bit. I wanted you to know that I'll keep looking into this. And I wasn't joking about the job either."

"I appreciate it. I just think the best solution would be—"

A sharp rap on the door interrupts me and wakes Oliver who looks confused and still half asleep. However, when he sees the delicacies on the table, an awed smile lights up his face.

"Courtney! Are you in there?" Rory demands.

Oh, shit. I'm not even dressed yet, and I'm having breakfast with Sienna Caruso. That won't go over well.

"I haven't changed my mind," I say. "I'm meeting my new boss tomorrow. Oliver and I can stay at his place."

"Nonsense. You pack your things and come back right now."

"I can't talk to you like that."

"I can," Sienna says and gets up.

"No, don't do that," I plead.

"Don't worry. I've taken precautions," she says. "You and Oliver are safe. You have my promise." Sienna marches straight to the door and yanks it open.

"Hi Rory. Long time no see. Did you come to talk about the incident at one of our resorts?"

So much for making peace. I can't believe what I'm hearing.

"What incident?" he asks irritably. "I sure as hell didn't come to talk to you. She's trying to withhold our grandson from us, and that's not right. You want to talk, Sienna, let's talk about one of our shipments that was confiscated by customs at the harbor last night."

"Is Grandpa mad?" Oliver whispers. He keeps close to me, and I can tell he's anxious. That is enough to make *me* mad.

"Enough you two. Get out, everyone. You sort out what you need to sort out, but I'm going to start my job tomorrow."

"Courtney." Sienna's tone is soft and entirely too seductive for the subject of the conversation. I can't deal with either of them right now. "I mean it. I'm going to call the police. They might be interested in talking to either one of you, I don't care. Just give me some room to breathe."

"We have more important things to do than to watch your shipments come in. I don't feel safe leaving her alone with you," Sienna snaps at Rory. "You go first."

In a huff, Rory leaves the room, not before threatening, "I'll be back. This isn't over, Courtney."

In the doorway, Sienna turns around, giving me a questioning look, a hopeful smile.

I shake my head.

"As you wish," she says and walks away. I lock behind both of them, wishing I had the time and space for a meltdown. Seeing that there are tears in Oliver's eyes, it's not going to happen anytime soon.

"We'll be okay," I promise him as I hug him close. "Let's pack and go on a little trip, okay?"

"Can we say goodbye to Jade and Sienna and Grandpa and Saoirse?"

"Of course we can, sweetie."

I don't even feel bad about lying. Maybe that's how it starts? All I know is that I need to get out of this place. Take stock of my mistakes and move on.

Chapter Sixteen

K evin Hollis had hoped this day would never come, though he wasn't naïve enough to believe it. The wild card was Sienna Caruso getting cozy with the prince's widow, which was intriguing, but also a major complication to his livelihood, and possibly, life.

Fortunately for him, he knew the players, and their stakes, inside out. In his job, he often came across the kind of lowlife that got hired as foot soldiers for mob families.

A little nudge here, a tidbit of information there, he could do it all without ever getting his hands dirty. Dirtier. Those were semantics as long as his wife was enjoying the life he was able to offer her, and his kids were gushing about all the amenities of their private school.

He had long decided he wasn't going to be the one who'd be taken advantage of, the cop in whose face criminals laughed when he arrested them. They both knew they'd be out in a heartbeat, and that they made more money than he would ever see in his lifetime.

Kevin knew he had to act fast when word got out that Sienna Caruso was inquiring about the witness the night of Tommy Flynn's death, and that she was frequently visiting Courtney Flynn's suite.

Working for men with egos bigger than houses had taught him many things, among them, that the egos of the people they employed were equally as inflated. In some cases, they feared the one at the top, but they would all fall over each other to tell the boss something was up. *The Carusos are planning something. Watch that shipment.*

Someone vandalized a Grand Palace resort? *Once you find the one responsible, look out for ties to Rory and his clan.*

So far, so good, he thought when he sat in his office after a meeting with the mayor who was concerned with the recent escalating events.

Escalation was good. It would take the heat off of him for a while. He sipped his coffee, making a grimace. Ironic that he was still drinking police station coffee when at home, he was enjoying the finest blends.

Most of the time, his job was to look the other way, and thus his conscience wasn't burdened much whenever these families executed their archaic dance. He had nightmares sometimes about Tommy Flynn's blood on his hands, but this wasn't his fault. It was a damn accident, one that no one could ever know about.

Better to be rich than to be dead and disgraced. The distraction had worked. Now he had to present alternative suspects. He had a few ideas.

Sienna

What the hell did he mean about the shipment? I take care of immediate matters first, which makes it easier to ignore that Courtney shut me out, literally and figuratively. I hate it, I don't know what to do about it, and it drives me crazy.

Hence, burying myself in work. Not that the recent incident and the daily business aren't giving me enough to do, but I still have to communicate with my source to get the bigger picture on the incident Flynn was talking about.

I hear what he has to say, and then I tell him to look a bit more into Hollis, and Saoirse Reilly. Something about her strikes me as very relevant to this story.

She's been around the Flynn family for a long time. Maybe even a Flynn hopeful, but then Courtney came along, and Tommy fell madly in love as they traveled together in Europe.

So much for escaping my state of relative, irritating, but real misery.

How did I ever let it get this far? I see things a lot clearer now that the haze of lust and affection has lifted some.

Make no mistake, I still have a lot of affection for her, and the son who didn't ask for any of it. It's so easy to reminisce, but I don't have the time to slip into a daydream of Courtney and me together, the rush of desire.

I struggle to admit it even to myself, because for most of my life, it was easy to cut ties. Nothing was more important than the ties to my family, the people I owe everything to.

But Francesco and Simona are hell-bent on believing that Courtney had darker motives for coming to town, that she and Rory were in on it from the beginning.

I've seen them together. I've heard what she said. There's no way she's implicated, and truth be told, I'm not even sure Rory is. That might be cutting him too much slack, but I'm just not sure.

Back to Saoirse Reilly. Easier to admit for me, I'd prefer the bad cop over the bodyguard, though I might be mistaken. Just because a woman knows how to take care of herself, it doesn't mean she's involved in something criminal. It doesn't mean she isn't. It's almost impossible to hang around the Flynns this long and not be involved in the action.

Murder, someone *in* the family, that's a whole other level but what if the rumors about her and Tommy were true? They spent a lot of time working closely together, on importing whiskey or extortion and intimidation, who knows.

What if she wanted more? What if he didn't, comfortable having a beautiful wife and his son, the Flynn heir, waiting for him at home? He already had everything, including, maybe, the mistress. I cringe at my own thoughts. This is why I would have liked her off the list. I don't accuse women just because of who they sleep with or want to sleep with. That would be highly hypocritical, wouldn't it?

Regardless, there is the possibility that she realized he was never going to leave Courtney and didn't like it. A woman with her skill set could get away with it. Either way, she was heartbroken over his death, and that could mean many things. Genuine grief over the loss of her lover. Guilt, because she was the one who shot him.

Nico being there that night, their almost rekindled friendship during the treacherous ceasefire, made it easy for the killer to offer an alternative suspect.

But it never stuck completely, the evidence not compelling enough.

I might not solve it today, but I want to keep an eye on all of them.

I want to call Courtney and ask her to meet, but I, too, have my pride, and my regular work to do.

Regular reports will have to do for now.

Chapter Seventeen

Courtney

Once again, Oliver and I get off a train, a half hour outside of the city. One of Will's employees is already waiting for us. He puts our luggage into the trunk of his car and then drives us through the hills to the place where we will stay for the foreseeable future.

Out here in the countryside, away from the drama, I can breathe a little easier, though it's bittersweet. It reminds me of when I first met Tommy, so unbelievably naïve, thinking I found family. I wonder if he had arguments with his father about protecting me from certain knowledge about their operations, when it's so clear that Rory and Ciara would have preferred Saoirse, who knows a whole lot more than I ever will.

Bittersweet, because I didn't mean to run, again, without talking to Sienna.

I can't get her off my mind, especially since she didn't deserve me yelling at her just because I was overwhelmed. I couldn't deal with the constant mutual accusations any longer, resulting in more drama, more danger, potentially death.

Taking Oliver out of all of this was still the right decision. I wish I could call her, but I assume she's busy with the aftermath of the vandalism, and I need to focus on the next steps. It was nice enough of Will to give me an extra day—I have to get Oliver and I settled, and tomorrow, finally, start my job.

The only silver lining of the chaos is that Rory and Saoirse have gone home for the time being. I have to figure something out before he takes the next step. Maybe I should call a lawyer.

Will is waiting for us at the reception counter.

"Hey, Courtney," he says, greeting me with a brief hug. "I'm so glad you could make it."

"That's not a joke, right? I'm sorry I had to reschedule on you."

"Things happen. But you're here now, right. And so is...You must be Oliver. Welcome to the Hillside Inn."

A bit shy, Oliver takes the outstretched hand.

"Thank you."

"I'm going to show you your room, and if you come find me after lunch, I can start to show you around. Oliver can come with us this time, and we'll figure something out until preschool starts."

"Thank you so much. I really appreciate this."

"I do too. You were always good with people. I think you're going to enjoy this."

I'm not sure what he remembers, but my track record hasn't been so good lately. Everyone I care about, except for my parents who are blissfully ignorant of it all, has kept the truth from me. I didn't see it. Didn't want to see it.

I'll have to do better. And once I know what I'm doing here, I'll see if Sienna still wants to talk to me.

Not just because she could help me find answers. There's something about her that doesn't let me go.

Oliver and I follow Will to our room. It's not quite as luxurious as the Grand Palace in the city, but it will do nicely until we find something more permanent. This will work. It has to. I can't imagine a life where we'd have to be on the run forever. The next time I speak to Rory and Ciara, they will understand that I won't try to keep Oliver from them, as long as they don't resort to threats.

"How do you like it here?" I ask Oliver as I pick him up and show him the view from our window. It's nice and calm, away from the bustling city. Not quite as remote as the mansion.

"It's nice," he says, but it sounds a bit like there's a question mark at the end.

"Yes, it is."

"Can we see Sienna? And—"

And Jade, and Grandpa, and Saoirse. I need to keep things simple for a bit.

"Soon," I promise, him, and me. At least where Sienna is concerned. I cannot speak for the others, so it's not quite a lie.

───ell───

After dinner, the day before my official start, I call Sienna. I wish I knew how to interpret her tone, friendly, but distant. Beneath it, I can find the woman who made me feel things I'd only fantasized about before. I'm still infatuated with her, and I curse all the complications that led us here, apart.

However, if I'd never left the mansion to sort out my growing concerns and suspicions about Rory's business, we might never have met. Not this way, anyway.

What's the solution?

"Did you figure out who drove the car into the hotel?" I finally ask.

"We haven't heard anything yet, but if the police are smart, they'll figure it out. There must have been evidence all over the place."

"Yeah. I imagine. Rory went home to deal with the shipment situation."

We are silent for a few seconds, before she asks, "Courtney, why did you call?"

I opt for brutal honesty.

"I wanted to hear your voice." Before she can react, I hasten to explain. "We haven't really had time to talk since...I mean...I'm sorry. I really am."

What else is she waiting for? Since we're going for honesty, we might as well go all the way. "I promise you I had nothing to do with whatever is going on right now. All I wanted was a safe space for Oliver and myself. I didn't plan for anything else."

"Neither did I. What are you saying?"

"Can I see you? I know you probably can't get away right now, but maybe for the weekend. I didn't mean to leave things like that."

"I can be there tomorrow," she says, and my knees go weak. "I might have a few more results for you as well. How are you and Oliver settling in?"

"Well, so far so good." I'm not sure whether to be relieved or disappointed. "Will told me Oliver can stay with me while I work, and I can get him into preschool here."

"So, it wasn't meant to be a dramatic exit?"

That hint of amusement puts a smile on my face. "No. Whatever Rory is or isn't doing, I don't think he ever wanted me to be a part of it. And I know that while he and Ciara want to see Oliver whenever possible, they aren't nearly that fond of me...I'll still be careful, but I think the distance will do all of us some good."

"Fools," she says. "Who wouldn't be fond of you?"

I am so glad I called.

The chaos has to end sometime.

———⁓———

I wake up early, get myself and a sleepy Oliver ready so we can have breakfast before my shift starts. The outgoing receptionist has agreed to come in for a day and show me everything I need, and after that, I'll be on my own. Given what my life has been like for the past few years, I think I can handle the job. Better yet, as I told Sienna, it puts some distance between me and my complicated family relations. Maybe, after we've been here for a while, Oliver and I can go see my parents. I am not considering changing coasts, but it would be nice to spend some time with them. The last time I saw them was at Tommy's wake.

Yes, I'd like to get together for a happier occasion. Whatever that will be, against all odds I still wish that could involve Sienna. But at least she'll be here in a few hours.

I can't wait.

Chapter Eighteen

S itting next to Rory Flynn in his office, Saoirse Reilly once more had the misfortune of listening to Hollis, the cop who had been sneaking around the business for almost a decade and gotten away with a substantial amount of money over time. In exchange for services rendered, for sure, but Saoirse thought he was overly dramatic, and single-minded in trying to get Rory even more enraged about the Carusos.

One Caruso in particular, who seemed to have corrupted Tommy's widow Courtney.

Tommy. She often wondered what he'd have to say about all this if he was still in their lives.

Contrary to popular belief, Saoirse had never had a torrid affair with the man whose life she'd been paid to guard. It wasn't for a lack of imagination.

She had cut her losses early and accepted that it wasn't realistic, especially after he brought home Courtney.

Courtney had to be protected at all costs, whether she wanted it or not. Well, it wasn't a question of whether she wanted it, because Tommy decided she was to stay blissfully ignorant about the darker side of liquor import. And while she stood up to everyone who got in her way, Saoirse had always had a hard time saying no to Tommy—so she kept an eye on Courtney too.

She and Tommy had been best friends since the 4th grade. They shared everything, including his concerns about his parents crossing lines when it came to doing business. He agreed to be a part of it anyway because that's what you did for family. It weighed on him. He was interested in forming alliances.

And now he was dead.

Saoirse wasn't feeling particularly beholden to the Flynns anymore, but she did hate bullies, always had, from the day she had punched a boy in school who made fun of Tommy for wearing glasses. In their adult lives, they had just become more powerful and dangerous, but she was still determined to take them on.

What happened to Rory and Ciara, first with the poisoned whiskey, then the murder of their son, and a few recent alarming events, went far beyond that.

Saoirse planned to stick around long enough to figure out who was behind those events and make them pay.

An eye for an eye can only work so long, Tommy had said.

It works as long as you're the one who has the last word, she had returned.

Saoirse was planning on having the last word. After that, she could finally move on.

Sienna

After assuring myself that everything is stable at home, I drive to the romantic small town outside of the city where Courtney plans to make a living for her and Oliver. It's charming all right, but I wonder if it's going to be permanent. Not just because I'm someone who needs the city to function. A little getaway every once in a while is fine.

Being out of the loop for too long makes me nervous, especially after all hell broke loose the last time I turned off my cell for a few hours. Underneath her desire to find some stability, I assume that the same might be true for Courtney.

It's a question to raise another day. As I drive along winding roads climbing the hills, I think back to the tirade Francesco gave me when we last spoke.

You can't trust anybody in that family.

Funny how the word family is spoken with reverence when it's your own, almost spat when it's them. There is so much meaning in those three syllables. A potential for a world of hurt.

I'm probably just tired from the past few days, years, if I'm honest. Excited to see her again. Worried that this is not the end, that Rory Flynn has decided it's time to fulfill irrational revenge fantasies.

I used to feel more responsible, like I was the only one who could and should fix it. But I am just one person running a multi-million-dollar business and making sure that all the numbers add up. Simona and Francesco used to respect that, but more and more it seems like they expect additional efforts from me, something to prove I won't sell them out to their archenemy. That was never an option, and it isn't now.

I left before discussing Hollis or Reilly with them, unsure that it was the right time to turn their wrath on either of them before we have more proof.

I keep going back to Hollis, the decorated cop. Is it realistic to think he simply made a mistake thinking it was Nico who shot Tommy that night? Something definitely doesn't fit, and I'm surprised no one has taken a closer look. Even Nico dutifully packed his bags and left the country when he could, and he is apparently not in a hurry to clear his name. Why is that?

Whatever the reason, I still can't and won't believe that he's the one who pulled the trigger. If anything, he has a bit of a romantic outlook, the lack of which made me perfect for running the boring part of the business.

I almost laugh to myself. Look where you are now. I'm skipping work in the middle of the week to spend time with the woman I'm...What, Sienna? Falling in love with? I don't do that. I can't.

I'm almost spooked enough to make a U-turn and head home, but then I don't, naïve or desperate, I don't know. Courtney asked me to come. One way or another, this means something for the two of us.

~ell~

Courtney steps out from behind the reception to hug me, and I drown in sensation, the warmth of her body, the scent of her perfume. It's comforting and scary alike. It can't last long either because she's still at work. Then it's Oliver, and when I pick him up and see the sweet surprise in his face, I must admit that I missed him too. I can't wait until Courtney is off and we can have dinner together.

"I'm sorry," she says with audible regret.

"It's okay. You just started the job. I can entertain myself until later. How about I check in, and then Olli and I go for a snack?"

"You would do that?"

"Of course. Just give me a few minutes."

Upstairs in the room I booked for the night, I change into more comfortable clothes, jeans and a light sweater, a pair of sneakers more appropriate for spending a few hours with a young child. Part of me is astonished that I haven't even questioned it, more so, that neither Courtney nor Oliver have. Jade, Saoirse Reilly, they are familiar.

I am still the stranger here, but they seem to feel safe with me, and that makes me feel...a bit odd. Oddly happy.

I come back down, smugly aware of the way Courtney's eyes widen when she sees me. She's dealing with a guest, so I have to wait a bit before she comes over to me.

"You look...different."

How could I have ever believed she might be scheming on behalf of her in-laws? Unlike me, she wears her heart on her sleeve. It's a quality I find puzzling but nevertheless intriguing.

"Can't say the same about you. You are your usual gorgeous self."

Predictably, the blush appears on her cheeks. "I didn't mean..."

"It's okay. Is the young man ready?"

"Yes, I am," Oliver quips excitedly.

Courtney smiles affectionately as she ruffles his hair. "You heard him. Please be careful, he's the only one I have."

I sense the deep, undeniable truth behind this. Family. Love. Loyalty, bonds that can be glorious and frightening, because there's always the fear of losing them.

"I'll be guarding him with my own life," I promise. "Let's go?"

"Can I have waffles?" he asks.

I look at Courtney, and we both have to laugh. "We'll see if we can find you some. I'm in the mood for something sweet myself."

I'm going to spoil him, but since it's only for the day, Courtney seems all right with it.

"There's a diner on main street, not far from here. I haven't been yet, but you might get lucky."

"We'll give it a try."

It's all been chaotic in my head, the work, the troubling incidents, Francesco and Simona seemingly unraveling. Or Rory Flynn, it's hard to tell at this point. I wish I could go back to a time when I felt like everything was under control.

And yet, I'm able to enjoy this moment of relative peace as Oliver and I make the short walk to the town's main street, where we indeed find the diner.

His small hand in mine, it's a strange yet welcome feeling.

There was a point in my life when I thought I'd go the mostly traditional route, find a woman to marry, have a child. Maybe, children, even. The demands of the business didn't leave any room for more than the occasional one-night-stand, or at least that's what I was telling myself. My family, no matter if they were more cynical or romantic about our circumstances and position in the business world, was fine with that.

It's no wonder that my aunt and uncle are questioning my actions. I would too, except I feel like I have earned some time, to take a step back and figure out what matters to me, beyond my penthouse office.

Listening to Oliver chat as we walk inside the diner, thinking of whatever else the next few hours could hold, I'm surprised by the ferocity of want, for that life outside the family business.

I think of all people, Courtney is the first to understand.

And I definitely wouldn't make her live with Francesco and Simona, because I value my own space just as much.

It's still all highly complicated, but the choices of a four-year-old are not.

Oliver's eyes grow wide when the server brings the coveted waffle, covered in fruit, chocolate sauce and a sprinkle of marshmallows. I have a moment of panic wondering if he's going to be sick.

"Thank you so much," he whispers in awe. "You can have some of it if you want."

"That's very generous of you. Thank you, Olli. Would you like to play a game?"

Chapter Nineteen

Courtney

I got it bad, and I can't deny it. Once my shift is done, I hurry to get us ready once again, a task prolonged by the fact that Oliver won't stop talking about how awesome his afternoon with Sienna was. They ate waffles—giant ones, judging by the fact that he's not hungry at all, and the picture Sienna sent. They also played some games, and *Sienna is so much fun!*

Yes, she is, I think, giddy. There hasn't been a lot of fun lately, and it's for him that I kept going. Knowing that Oliver is so easily accepting of her, that she's so good with him, puts me in a dangerous state. Hopeful. I have a job, an amazing kid, a woman who cares enough to drop everything to come see me.

I couldn't ask for more. Things couldn't be better, could they? That question is tempting fate, so I push it aside. Finally, we are ready to meet Sienna in the lobby. There are guests going about their business, Will in the vicinity, and yet she kisses me right there, in a way that leaves no doubt about the relationship we share.

No one blinks an eye. Here I'm just Courtney, not the woman who somehow became attached to a name with a complicated reputation.

"I'm so glad you're here," I say.

"Me too!" Oliver pipes up.

She smiles, that enigmatic smile that drew me to her right away, a warmth to it now.

"Me too."

I haven't had time to explore the town a lot, testimony to how I fled from one city, and then another, but I know there's an Italian restaurant on the corner. They have a table for us.

"I was afraid you might not be hungry either," I joke, making her laugh.

"Oh I am."

That's almost a bit more innuendo than I can handle, making me much aware of the warmth gathering...well, in my heart and elsewhere.

Sienna easily switches from the lascivious subject to a more practical one. "I know it's early, but how do you like working here?"

"It's relaxed," I say. "Pretty much what I had hoped. And much more relaxed than being at home." I lower my voice on the last few words. I have to give it to Rory and Ciara, if they wanted to put pressure on Oliver, he certainly didn't feel any of it. No, the pressure was all mine, knowing that someday, it would be on him—and if I let it be, then that someday, it might be too late.

"So you'll stay in one place for a while. That's good to know."

"You can come see us any time you want."

Oliver hasn't been this chatty in a while, I notice. I can't help smiling. The three of us at this table, in this moment, it's too good to be true. It almost feels like...family.

I've been angry and bitter about this having been taken away from me, from Tommy. Part of me still is. It's ironic, and in a sense, poetic, that I'm here with the woman Rory has accused of being the villain for a long time. Poetic. Justice will have to wait until we know more. I'm kind of curious, but I also don't want to discuss this in front of Oliver. That, and I'm not completely unselfish, wanting to stay in this cozy bubble for a while.

"Thank you," she tells him. "I'm glad to hear that." Her eyes meet mine, an unspoken question in them. Here, in this place, we are so far away from the innuendo, the doubts, the demands of others.

"I second the sentiment," I say.

I'm a bit less amused, later, when she confesses about showing pictures to Oliver during their outing.

"What the hell!" I'm pacing in the small bathroom while she's leaning against the door. "Every time I trust you, when I think this is something real..."

"It is," she interrupts me. "Believe me, this, whatever this is between us, is the most real thing about it. And he clearly wasn't traumatized by a few questions about who's coming and going at your in-laws' house."

I have a hard time arguing with that. During dinner, Oliver finally found a bit of appetite again, and he nodded off before we made it back to the room, his sleep undisturbed. My point still stands. I think.

"Regardless. It wasn't up to you."

"Maybe, but I think you want this to end as much as I do. Rory going home, the same for Nico, I believe it would be the best for Oliver if we all stopped trying to one-up each other."

"That's a strange way to talk about murder."

"But I didn't murder anyone, and you know that." Even though we speak in hushed tones, the heat comes through clearly in her words. "You know that, Courtney."

I do, my breath catching in my throat as she steps into my personal place. Something about her changing demeanor, hot and cold, powerful businesswoman, passionate lover, calls to me like nothing else.

"Someone *did* murder Tommy."

"My point exactly. This cop, Hollis, he came to your house often enough for Oliver to remember him. What kind of witness is he? His boss or colleagues might have backed him up, but I'm telling you, I've had my people looking into him, and something is off."

"Your people." And here we are again, though her hand on my arm is distracting. I make myself listen for any sounds from the bedroom, but it's quiet. No distraction. No way out.

"Yes, my people, because with what we do, we need adequate security, and we need information. Hollis has been spending a lot of money on property and private schools for his kids. He comes from money, but not that much."

This is giving me a headache.

"But what would be the point? Let's say Rory has funneled money to him for favors, not that I would know anything about it, why would he say Nico shot Tommy? Or, if you think he did it, same question—why?"

"That, I don't know yet." I can tell she's as frustrated as I am. "All I'm saying is that something doesn't add up."

Sienna has a point. Or several. I'm tired, still hoping that I have found a place where Oliver and I can stay for a while, but I can't deny it would help to know the truth.

"Will it ever end?"

Sienna lays her hands on my waist, lightly pulling me closer.

"Yes," she says with utmost conviction. "I promise." Then she leans in to kiss me, and even though my entire body gravitates towards her, I try to stop her. "We can't. Not now."

"Oh, we can."

Her smile tells me that she sees right through me, her fingers dancing just above the waistline of my pants. "We just have to be quiet...and quick."

"Sienna," I say, but it sounds like a plea. It might be one. I missed her, her knowing touch, the way she seems to instinctively know what I need, even if I'm hesitant.

"Courtney," she whispers against my neck, fingers sliding below the fabric to find naked skin. I bite my lip when they waste no time, brushing, teasing, pressing. Quick won't be a problem. Quiet might be, but I'll guard that bit of responsibility. "You'll be fine. I got you."

Oh, she does. Sienna makes quick process of the zipper and then her hand is back beneath the fabric of my panties, warm, demanding, making me shiver with lust and the need for release.

"This is crazy," I manage, the words tumbling out in a breathless gasp. It is also pure pleasure, glorious. I want her so much. I want this between us to work out, for so many reasons, but right at this moment I need her like this, inside me, all around me, bringing me to a scorching climax, effortlessly, it seems like. I hold on to her when I can barely stand, delighting in the continuing fireworks.

The bedroom is still quiet. I lick my lips, taking in the smug satisfaction on her face. I'm pretty sure I can make it even better.

In one quick move, I pull down her jeans with her panties and get to my knees.

"You said it had to be quick?"

She leans back against the sink, her fingers tightening on the edge.

"You think you can do that?"

"Let's find out," I say, running my hands over her thighs.

Eventually, her hands find their way into my hair, pulling a tiny bit, but I don't mind.

Maybe freedom is not a complete illusion, for me, or for her.

Chapter Twenty

Sienna

I feel accomplished after having avoided a potential catastrophe, and steering Courtney back to a more enjoyable place than the argument we almost had.

I stand by my word. She matters most of all—and I don't even stop and think how I got there. But Oliver matters to me too, his safety, and he was fine telling me about the times the man visited Grandpa Rory between mouthfuls of waffle.

It's interesting to think that people like Reilly and Hollis have been constants in his life too. We should take a harder look at Hollis. Bribes are almost a given. But Courtney has a point wondering why he would accuse Nico. To stir things up? To hide his own failure? If he was supposed to watch Tommy Flynn that night, and Tommy got killed anyway, Hollis would have one hell of a problem, except if he was the one to find the guilty party and bring them to justice.

But he hasn't. He has neither found the real culprit, nor gotten to his scapegoat, my cousin who's been enjoying life in and around Naples.

I can't help thinking that if we figure out what his deal is, finally, we'd get ourselves out of this mess. Rory isn't that patient.

Perhaps I could have tried to reason with him, but the way he was talking to Courtney still pisses me off.

At least, we have a few more hours to ourselves. She was surprisingly shy when we returned to the bedroom after our encounter in the bathroom but allowed me to stay.

And now I'm close to being overwhelmed by affection which is why I'm thinking about Hollis in the dead of night. I don't want to be the one constantly having to deal with crises, but there's no denying I have a knack for it.

Falling in love, to me, is a crisis of its own, but I can't stop it either. And I'm liking it too much to try.

ele

I slip out of bed early in the morning and head over to my own room where I get dressed and check my messages.

According to my investigator, Saoirse had an argument with Rory about Hollis and is off to a yet unknown location. It's strange that Rory seems to trust this man—but maybe he doesn't. Keep your friends close, your enemies closer, and if you can't tell yet which is which, don't let them out of your sight. I get the general idea.

I let it slide for the moment and catch up on some emails before I send a text to Courtney.

She will have to work, but I hope to have breakfast with her before I leave.

Courtney answers right away.

You were gone quickly.

I'm just downstairs in the breakfast room. Would you like to join me?

I'd like that very much, she replies, with a heart emoji. I still smile at the screen, when she and Oliver come down to join me at the table.

"Sorry. We were running a bit late," she says.

"Did you sleep well? You seemed...exhausted last night." I get the desired reaction, have her a bit flustered. Not missing a beat, I continue, "Good morning, Oliver. What about you?"

"So well! No bad dreams," he confirms, and for a moment I wonder if that is something frequent. Courtney's expression is unreadable.

"Any sleep without bad dreams is a good one. Are you hungry?"

He nods enthusiastically.

"Great. Then we should all attack the buffet, what do you say?"

Chapter Twenty-One

Courtney

I didn't tell her about the messages yet, all concerning, all intruding on my peaceful new start. Maybe it was imaginary, but as long as I'm doing my job, and Sienna and Oliver are both here with me, and safe, I can still pretend.

Sienna will have to leave before noon, but she's taken the time for a swim in the pool this morning. I don't join her, and I don't tell her why either. It seems irrelevant in the great scheme of things, something to figure out later.

Saoirse wants to meet me. I'm not sure if that's a good idea, or a terrible one. Or a trap.

Rory is angry and determined.

I stand outside the window to the pool area, the smell of chlorine nearly making me gag. It's not that, I know, but the fact that it's associated with the constantly moving water. Deep water. Cold. I shudder and turn away, it's all I can do not to yell at her to get out. Not that she'd hear me through the glass. I need to get back to work.

Sienna waves, and I decide that I'll tell her before she leaves. Not about the water though.

I'm back behind the reception area when she wheels her suitcase to the checkout counter.

"Did you enjoy your stay?" I ask, trying for flirtatious, when I really want to cry. More messages. More accusations. The peace that filled me with so much hope is fleeting. So is the hope that we could reason with anyone in this chaos.

"Very much. I'll recommend it," she says with a wink. "I think I enjoyed the receptionist most of all."

I try to smile, but then the tears just fall, another guest giving me a puzzled glance.

"Courtney? What's wrong?"

She takes my arm and pulls me aside as Will steps in.

"Saoirse wants to see me," I say, even though I'm certainly not crying over her request. "I didn't want to make you worry, but I think Rory is planning something. To make me look like an unfit mother of something..." So much for being open-minded and understanding that I might not want to spend my life alone. But he warned me about getting involved with a Caruso.

I am terrified. And angry. It all seems so childish.

"I know about Saoirse," Sienna says to my surprise. "She and Rory seem to have had a falling-out, now he's taking it out on you. We won't let that stand."

I appreciate the sentiment, but what would we do?

"Mommy, what's wrong?" Oliver asks, tears in his eyes as well. Oh, damn it.

"It's fine. I'm fine," I repeat, wiping my face. "We're just going to miss Sienna, right?"

"But she's coming back. I definitely will," she promises as Will comes over.

"Is everything all right?" he asks, concerned.

I'm beyond embarrassed. I used to be independent, capable. How did I get here?

"Yes. I'm really sorry."

"Could you watch Oliver for a few minutes?" Sienna asks. "Not more, I promise, but I need to have a word in private with Courtney."

"Of course."

He might be my boss, but Sienna's authority is undeniable.

"I don't know what's gotten into me," I say when we have that moment of relative privacy, still close enough so we can see him talk to Oliver. "I'm so sorry." My face is still burning, confusion, shame, other yet unnamed emotions. I've been holding it together for so long, I just assumed I always would.

"No need," she says, squeezing my arm gently. "I'm afraid I still have to go, but I'll keep in touch, and I'll be back as soon as possible." Leaning closer, she adds, "The bathroom situation might not be ideal, but I think we made it work."

I can't help smiling at that.

"Maybe it could be helpful to hear what Saoirse has to say but wait until the weekend when I can go with you. Rory, you don't have to answer him as long as he keeps yelling at you. We'll figure something out together."

"I need to get back to work. And thank you."

Sienna leans forward until our foreheads touch, staying there for a second or two before she kisses me softly.

"Thank you, Courtney. For more than you'll ever know."

With these cryptic words, she leaves, and I have to pull myself together.

Something will change, one way or another.

After apologizing to Will and settling Oliver back with his toys and coloring book, I pick up where I left off earlier, and fortunately, the guests from earlier are gone.

Despite my small meltdown, I feel better and more determined than ever. I'll hear Saoirse out, whatever it is she has to say. And I'll face Rory eventually. If he wants a fight, he has no idea what's coming to him.

I've never realized before how much of myself I had lost, when I stopped asking questions, curbed my curiosity for peace's sake, because Tommy thought it was better that way. It isn't all on him—after we moved into the mansion, I slipped into that role easily. When he was murdered, I became too afraid to ask questions, unable to deal with anything besides making sure Oliver was taken care of. That is still my priority. The implications of what Tommy and his family have likely been involved in for a long time, are still staggering, scary.

I will deal with it somehow, for Oliver's sake, and for mine.

I might be sleeping with the enemy, according to Rory, but the fact is that being with Sienna gave me that part of myself back.

I need to know.

And I need to stay here for a while, even if Sienna thinks I should come work for her, in the city. It's not about hiding. It's about figuring out, for good, who I really am.

Chapter
Twenty-Two

"Can you tell me why Courtney is starting to doubt your testimony? I need the truth, Kevin."

Rory Flynn might have used the same conversational tone as usual, but Hollis understood that being summoned to the mansion like this, in the middle of the day, was anything but.

"How would I know? I'm sure the Caruso woman put that in her mind."

"Because they want to point the guilt away from them, don't they?"

He was sweating now. "It's what they always do, and you know it. Perhaps they want Nico to come home and take over for her. I saw what I saw, no matter who has been doubting it. Nico shot Tommy. I saw him run away. You're not taking her word over mine, are you?"

"Please, Kevin, don't tell me whose word I should take. She's still the woman Tommy married, who gave us Oliver. She would have had the chance to do damage..."

"And maybe she did," Hollis blurted out. "Do you really know what she told Caruso? They could be in it together, planning run away with your grandson."

Rory actually laughed at that, a sound that grated on his nerves.

"Courtney is smarter than that. She knows we would find her, and besides, Sienna Caruso would never give up her business. Not for anyone, but certainly not for someone whose name is Flynn." His expression turned serious again. "I want to know who's behind those rumors, and if it wasn't Nico Caruso who pulled the trigger, who did it instead."

"I told you, it was him! As for the rumors, I'm on it."

"Work faster," Rory Flynn grumbled. "I pay you enough. And make the arrangements I've asked for."

"I will."

His heart was still hammering even as he sat in his car, miles away from the Flynns' property. Kevin Hollis wanted a drink badly, but he had arrangements to make. On behalf of Rory, and some of his own.

Apparently, the recent incidents hadn't been enough. He needed to step up his game.

And all roads, as it seemed, led back to the same person.

Sienna

The rest of the day feels almost normal, almost old me, though I can't deny the major changes. I'm doing my work as is expected of me, but every once in a while, my mind wanders back to the weekend, Courtney, the truths and the possibilities.

She has arranged the meeting with Saoirse. While I'm beyond curious about what the woman has to say, I can't wait to go back. Maybe figure out why Courtney never wants to join me in the pool. It's not just that. I want to know everything about her.

But before we can safely explore these ideas, there's other knowledge I need.

Kevin Hollis came into a lot of money about a decade ago, and he keeps spending it. I finally see it fit to raise my concerns with Francesco and Simona over dinner.

They give each other a startled look.

"Kevin Hollis?" Francesco repeats. "I doubt he wanted to shoot Tommy. He's a weasel, but he's much too afraid of Rory to pull something like that. No, I think he was supposed to watch him, failed, and came up with a story. Courtney Flynn—"

"Don't start," I warn. "This has nothing to do with her. All she wants is a future for herself, and her son. That's not too much to ask for."

"Maybe it is if you married a Flynn," Simona scoffs. "You can't tell me she never knew anything. They've been encroaching on our territory, working to destroy our reputation for years. How can you stand to be in the same room as her?"

"Simona." I am astonished, and disgusted. I have no regrets whatsoever regarding what happened when we were in the same room. Sure, the Flynns have been a pain, but there are nuances. Tommy, Saoirse, and most of all Courtney...Not everyone is equally to blame for the ongoing battle.

"What? You are not going to choose her over us?"

It's late, and we've all had a bit of wine. With recent incidents, tempers have been running high. I get all that, but I have the bad feeling that there's more to it.

"I trust that you won't make me choose. It's been a long day. I should go home."

"Sienna!" Francesco thunders when I get to my feet and walk out of the room. "There are still things we need to discuss."

I hold up a hand without turning around.

"Tomorrow."

The same advice I gave Courtney is true for me too. I don't need anyone yelling at me.

—ele—

The next few days pass quietly, though the more I learn about Hollis' finances and regular visits to the Flynn mansion, the more concerned I am. Saoirse leaving is significant, and we can't learn soon enough about her reasons.

Or whatever else she knows.

144

It's important we talk to her before Rory finds her—or the authorities.

However, when I talk to Courtney in the evening via videochat, I don't focus on possible dire scenarios. I wish she could be here with me. I wish we'd have a moment to ourselves, where I could tell her, no, show her, I have a lot more to offer her than playing detectives together. Uncovering the truth, it matters, but I've had another long day, and from the looks of it, so has she.

Uncovering *her* would be a whole lot more pleasant, but we have work to do first.

"Get this. My aunt and uncle told me that Hollis provided them with information sometimes. So, he's playing both sides, because I'm convinced Rory doesn't know about this. If he did..." I let the words hang in the air.

"You don't have to be subtle about it," she says with a sigh. "I'm starting to get an idea of what they are capable of."

"This will all be over soon." I want to believe it. I want her to believe it. "Once we figure this out, Rory will understand that he needs to clean his own house first, and perhaps do some grieving instead of making wild accusations. And he'll understand that Oliver belongs with you, regardless of who you are married to."

Just for a second, I wonder if she's picked up on the possibilities hidden in this sentence, but like me, she's tired, and her mind is on other things.

"Thank you." And, with a hint of curiosity, she adds, "Are you suggesting I might marry again someday?"

In the midst of this turmoil, given that we've just met, the thought is downright ridiculous, but exciting at the same time. Francesco and Simona would never give their blessing, but after everything I've given to the business for almost thirty years, why would I care?

I owe them. I always will. That doesn't mean I can't have a life of my own. Does it?

"What's on your mind?" Courtney asks quietly. "You looked lost in thought for a moment."

"So many questions. And why wouldn't you marry again? You're young, attractive, and have the most adorable child. Who wouldn't want to be married to you?"

The words come out the way I want them to, matter-of-fact, a hint of amusement, nothing to reveal my state of mind. I'm good at that too.

"That's nice of you to say. I guess I'll revisit the idea when I can be sure Rory won't send his associates after me. Or when your family stops believing I conspired with him and Ciara, or that I seduced you for some intel."

"I agree, that's a preposterous idea. We both know who seduced whom."

She laughs at that. "I'm sorry, but I'm too exhausted to do this now. I can't wait to see you."

"Same here. I'll come to the inn, we'll meet Saoirse at the restaurant, and after that, we'll sort out the rest?"

"I'll have a babysitter for that night," she confirms. "Will's younger sister is home from college. He will be able to start preschool next week."

"Looks like things are going well."

"For the most part, they are. I'm really grateful," she says, her tone serious. "To Jade and Will, it goes without saying. Most of all, you."

My face heats at her statement.

"I haven't done much, in comparison."

"Without you, I might have caved the moment Rory came to town. I didn't want to, but he has a way of playing my guilt, and of course I don't want all those arguments in front of Oliver."

"Understandable."

"I felt like I was losing my mind, trying to put two and two together, the business, the people that came to the house, all the things Tommy didn't tell me. It all makes a lot more sense."

"I'm not innocent either," I feel the need to say. Just in case, one day, she brings up marriage again. I wouldn't repeat Tommy Flynn's mistakes. With me, Courtney would know what she's in for, whatever that means these days.

It certainly doesn't seem to mean as much any longer as I thought, not as much as she means to me.

"I know that. And I trust you. I have an idea how far you're willing to go for the ones you care about—and for the truth. I'm not sure I ever knew that with Tommy."

"I'm sorry. And I guess we'll find out."

"Yeah. One more thing—Oliver insists you'll have waffles together again."

"That's no problem. As long as you're with us."

So, we couldn't do anything racy in the video conference, but her having a babysitter bodes well for my weekend plans. And I don't mind having a family breakfast the next day either.

Definitions are changing. Against all odds, I welcome it.

***

What I don't welcome is the car that keeps following me when I drive out to Courtney's place the next day. It's hard for them to hide their intention after we leave the city traffic. They stay two cars behind, but at some point, we are out on more rural roads, and then it's just them and me.

A man, I believe. I get a glimpse of the license plate and save it to my phone with voice to text. Meeting with the long-time bodyguard of the Flynn family, I came of course armed. I don't want any complications with Courtney around.

I keep my eye on the car. Its driver stays behind me, but they don't make a move. It's not Hollis. It could be one of Flynn's. At this point I'm not sure that one of my own wouldn't send someone to observe me. Or it's Saoirse behind all this. What game is she playing?

I find myself driving faster. Even though I'm going to pick up Courtney at the inn where she's in relative safety, something tells me it's important to get there as soon as possible.

By now, word has likely gotten around that she took the job at the Hillside Inn.

And Oliver is there too.

Someone could try...I glance over to the gun visible in my open purse. No, not on my watch.

Chapter
Twenty-Three

Courtney

Given how excited Oliver is to spend the evening with Will's sister Alice, I'm beginning to wonder if my worries were more about me than him. He's a champion, dealing with all the changes so well, ready to open up to the world.

Am I? Ready to be out here, to make a living, to trust someone to get close? I want to believe I am, but the more time I spend away from the mansion and Tommy's family, the more I have to acknowledge uncomfortable truths as well. Maybe I was hiding away there too. Rory and Ciara let me, not because they liked me so much, but because it meant Oliver was always around.

And I can be fairly certain now that they had, perhaps still have, plans for him that go far beyond private school.

He seems fine to move on, and so should I.

Still, as I get ready for an evening of confessions, putting on some make-up, I'm aware of my heart beating fast, my hands shaky to the point that I'm doing a terrible job. I frown at my mirror image, thinking that this will have to do.

Several people owe me the truth, let's start with one who probably knew more about Tommy than I ever will. Somehow, it's not that fact that's making me nervous.

I get up and glance at my watch, shaking my head at my rumbling stomach. I'm not sure I will even be able to eat, but my body seems to have other ideas.

There's no turning back now. Sienna will be here in less than an hour, and then, maybe, we'll finally learn the truth.

─ele─

I'm pacing the length of the room, checking my phone again. Sienna's last text confirmed that she was on her way. I haven't heard from her since.

Don't be late, Saoirse told me when we agreed on a meeting place. Neutral territory. I could go by myself if Sienna was held up by anything? I hope she'll be on time, and not just for this curious encounter. I have no idea what the aftermath will look like.

I jump when my phone rings.

"I'm still in my room. Where are you?" I ask.

"I know where you are," the voice says, making my blood run cold. I remember that voice. I haven't heard it in a while, but it can't be a coincidence that he's calling me right at this moment. Sienna's inquiries. Saoirse's sudden departure from the family, and the mounting suspicions.

"What do you want?"

"Why don't we talk about what you want, Courtney? I'm sure keeping your son safe is high on that list."

Just like that, the ground crumbles underneath me, just for a few seconds, because if I'm honest, I've always known this moment would come.

I always thought Rory would challenge me, try to take Oliver away from me, but he's not the only one who knows they can get to me through my son.

I don't allow myself more than a moment of panic. I know I have to think clearly now, follow the logical next steps. Mixed in with the fear is a mindless anger, for men like him who think they can use people to cover up for their own mistakes. Children, for God's sake.

"I want him back. That's all I care about. Let me speak to him."

"Not yet," he says.

"How do I know you're not bluffing?"

He gives a bitter laugh. "You really want to take that risk? Why don't you check with your babysitter? She hasn't texted you an update in a while, has she?"

"What did you do to her?"

"Nothing. Yet. Send her a text and you'll see she won't be answering."

"Why are you doing this?"

"Stop asking questions," he huffs. "You're wasting time. Go straight to this address. You do it now, or you'll never see him again." As if reading my mind, he adds, "I have eyes on you, Courtney. Don't call anyone, I'll know if you do, and we'll disappear. I swear I'm serious."

I am too. He's going to pay for this. I think of Oliver, who has just barely started opening up to a world beyond the mansion, with kind, gentle people. Jade. Will. Sierra. Even Saoirse cares in her own way.

If it's not Rory behind this, what does it mean? Has Hollis lost it?

In any case, he has Oliver. I need to act now.

"Did you get that?"

"Yes. I'm on my way."

Is he really watching me? I can't say for sure, can't take the risk, especially if he's screening my calls somehow. He's a cop, a crooked one at that. I'm sure that if he wanted to, he could.

I won't take any risks with my son's life.

My mind is clear now, my hands steady when I sit behind the wheel.

Did he put a camera in my car?

Get that, asshole. You're not going to get away with this. I don't say it out loud, for the fear that he could hear me.

I pray that Sienna will understand something is very wrong when she doesn't find me at the inn. Otherwise, I'm running out of back-up plans.

How did everything happen so fast? I'm worried about Alice. If Sienna and I are right, Hollis has already killed. I can't even allow a sliver of all those emotions battling for the lead in my brain. I need to be as cold and calculating as the corrupt cop. One of us might not make it out, and it can't be me. For Oliver and Alice's sake, it can't be me.

I find the address Hollis gave me, a surprisingly well-kept neighborhood given the circumstances. It is a remote area by the lake, houses of wealthy owners. It makes me sick to think that this man has been living in luxury because of running errands for the Flynns. I had hoped Tommy was never involved in any of it, but I doubt it now.

Sienna might have employed a few illegal business practices of her own. I can't think about this, can't doubt her.

First, I have to find Oliver, bring him home.

That's my only priority right now.

—*ele*—

I have barely parked when Hollis appears out of the blue, wearing black pants and a black hooded sweatshirt. I try to guess his state of mind, but his expression is neutral, not giving anything away. He won't waver. This is not some last resort action. He, too, had a Plan B.

He's pointing the gun at my window.

"Get out of the car!"

He's one of those people who clearly enjoy the power his job gives him—even though he's a disgrace for said job. He has also enjoyed the relative power and money that comes with being on the take. I'm almost certain that he considers Oliver merely a pawn in this stupid, childish game, but I can't care. Logical next steps.

I obey, and he spins me around, slamming me against the side of the car before he puts the cuffs on me. Of course. A blindfold is next.

"I did what you said. Where is Oliver?"

He might just want to get rid of everyone who has ever raised suspicions against him, and in his position, he might get away with it. Several seconds tick by when I can hardly breathe.

"You'll see him soon," he says.

"And then what? You're going to kill us both?"

He steers me away towards another vehicle, and into the passenger seat, his reaction to my question an amused chuckle. As if I said something funny. I hate this man for bringing Oliver into this. At the core of it all, he's a coward.

"You got that wrong. I don't kill anybody. Other people might, but I don't think Rory hates you that much. He just wants to be a Grandpa, you know?"

"I don't think I got it wrong. You murdered Tommy, right? Why did you do it? Did he find out that you were selling out the family?"

"Look who's talking, the girl who couldn't get herself and her son far enough away from the family. Don't give me that bullshit. You never cared, that's why you weren't initiated into the finer details of Flynn Import."

"I know enough," I say as he fastens my seatbelt—how fucking considerate—and drives away. "You told everyone that Nico Caruso shot Tommy, because you knew it was going to earn you points with Rory. And it worked, because Caruso fled the country which made him look guilty."

"You have no idea what you're talking about."

I feel the sting of a needle—less considerate now—and I can only imagine he doesn't want the conversation. The world is already black behind the blindfold, and I slip into nothing.

Chapter Twenty-Four

S o far, so good. The plan had worked, the first, crucial part of it, anyway. For Kevin Hollis, it wasn't time yet to relax and get on with his life. The next phase was equally important.

Rory picked up on the fourth ring. He didn't consider Hollis all that important these days, but that would change, not just because Saoirse Reilly had fled the ship.

"I hope this is important," Flynn grumbled. "I don't have much time."

For once, he would make the time. And listen.

"I'm afraid I have bad news. Courtney...she's gone. The Carusos have her."

"What are you talking about?" Rory Flynn sounded dumbfounded. "What do you mean, they have her? She's sleeping with that woman."

"Yes, but something must have gone wrong there. Maybe they broke up. In any case, she's in danger. What do you want me to do?"

"Did she have Oliver with her?"

A hint of anxiety was creeping into the man's tone. Now, they were getting somewhere.

"I'm still trying to figure that out. So…"

"Find him, and bring him here," Rory commanded. "What did she expect, getting mixed up with these people? I want him safe."

"I'll do what I can."

"No, you didn't hear me correctly. I want *him* safe. Can you do that, or do I have to call Saoirse?"

Well, good luck with that. Sarcasm wasn't first and foremost on his mind. He was sweating.

"What about Courtney?"

"Are you really that stupid? I don't give a damn about her. She made her bed when she left us. I want my grandson. Find him and bring him home. You let me know when it's done."

"Yes, of course."

As he ended the call, he cast a look at the still unmoving figure on the bench. As usual, he had recorded the conversation, not that this one would do him any good. Damn it all. Not only did he have to figure out a way to bring Oliver to Rory, but he also had to get rid of her as well.

First, he had one more call to make.

Sienna

I 'm late, and the moment I enter the lobby and don't see Courtney, I know she didn't listen to me. I suppress a curse and walk up to the desk where her friend Will is still working.

"Hi. Have you seen Courtney?"

He gives me a puzzled look. "I thought you were going to meet with her? She left half an hour ago." Casting a look at his watch, he corrects himself. "Closer to an hour. Is everything all right?"

"I hope so," I mumble, turning and heading back to my car. If anything, Saoirse Reilly leaving the Flynn clan is a good thing. I don't think that she wants to do Courtney harm, but someone who does might be watching both of them. My call goes to voicemail.

I'm speeding on the way to the restaurant, fortunate that I don't run into the cops. The last thing I need now is a situation where I have to explain myself. Briefly, I consider employing our family's resources, but I've done it quite a bit, and with what we've planned tonight, it's tricky. I might come back to that.

I park the car on the curb and jog up the stairs to the front door. Rushing past a dumbfounded hostess, I find a bored looking Saoirse at a table on the far end of the room. She has a glass of water and a menu in front of her.

"Hey there. Is it finally time for drinks?"

"Where the hell is Courtney?"

"How would I know? She agreed to meet me here. I've been waiting."

"You haven't heard from her?"

"Not since she confirmed the time and place. What's going on?"

She's a cool customer, but I have a pretty good radar for when someone is trying to bullshit me. I'm certain she's telling the truth.

"I don't know yet. She was supposed to wait for me at the inn. She's not picking up her phone. Tell me, do you have any idea who could be behind this?"

Saoirse shrugs. "If it's no one from your family, and not Rory who wants to bring them back to the family, I wouldn't know."

"Why would it be anyone from my family?" I return, irritated. "They know we're dating. They might not like it, but they won't touch her. The fact that you're here and not at the Flynns' mansion any longer tells me that Rory is a more likely candidate."

"Maybe," she contends. "Him, or freaking Kevin Hollis. That man gets on my nerves."

"Hollis? Why do you think that?"

I'm trying not to panic. If Hollis is behind this, and he feels cornered, there's no saying how far he might go.

"Because he's a pain in the ass, and he's been playing both sides for some time now. Dangerous game, but apparently, he's been getting away with it so far. Rory taking his word over mine was the last straw."

"Come on," I say.

"What?"

Isn't it obvious?

"We have to find Courtney. She is likely in danger."

"May I remind you I'm no longer part of any of this?"

"You've got to be kidding me. You won't help her because you were pining for her husband? No desire to bring down the man who did it?"

"Wait a minute."

She is on her feet, anger burning in her eyes.

"Do you have proof?"

"Circumstantial," I say. "It doesn't matter. You help me find her, and I'll buy you that drink that you crave so much."

With a somewhat exaggerated sigh she follows me.

"All right. Courtney's cool. I don't want anything to happen to her. I just want you to promise me one thing."

"What is that?"

"If Hollis murdered Tommy, you let me get to him first?"

"Sure. Let's go."

At this point I would have promised anything, because I know her expertise on the Flynn family and their involvement with Hollis is crucial. Will I keep that promise?

We'll see. If he hurt Courtney, or Oliver, all bets are off.

Something is definitely off. Courtney would never stay out of reach that long. We don't have much time, the knowledge sitting in my chest heavy and cold.

I'm grateful to have a partner, albeit an unwilling one, who can keep her cool.

Her investment is on a much different scale. Maybe Rory will welcome her back if she plays her cards right, maybe she doesn't care. None of it matters to me. I need to find Courtney, and I'm afraid for that, we first need to find Hollis.

"Can you contact him now?"

"I can try, but he's never particularly answered to me," she says, making a grimace. "Old school, you know?"

"Yeah. I know the type. So where do we find him?"

She's already on the phone. "Let's start with his work. We go from there."

Chapter Twenty-Five

Courtney

I am roused by a voice in the distance, and a strange sloshing sound. When I open my eyes, my vision blurs for a moment, and I have to fight nausea. I force myself to take slow, measured breaths. I am no longer wearing the blindfold, and my wrist is now cuffed to a ring hook in the wall, just low enough so I can't get all the way up.

My jaw drops when I realize where I am, and the waves of nausea return.

Oliver! I can't lose consciousness again or get sick. I need to get out of here. The sloshing sound comes from waves, only a few feet away. I'm in a boathouse, and that's entirely much too close to the lake. I can tolerate pools behind a door and large bodies of water when I'm far enough from them, but that doesn't seem to be Hollis' plan.

What if he never had Oliver, and I went into his trap without a second thought?

What if...

But why would he want just me, when it's so painfully clear that neither Tommy's family, nor Sienna's, has any respect for me? None of it makes sense, especially the part where he might make me go on that freaking boat.

I can't.

Since the day I was bullied in first grade and, while on a field trip, Terry Dawson pushed me into a lake when I hadn't yet learned to swim, I have successfully avoided any situation where I might drown. I'd much prefer to keep it that way, but what if Alice and Oliver are on the other side of that lake? There's certainly road access to wherever he's holding them, but that might take too long.

"Hollis!"

I try to call, my voice a pathetic croak. It makes me mad as well, and I yank on the restraint, making the cuff clank against the metal hook.

The distant one-sided conversation floating over to me tells me he's still on the phone, and judging from his agitated tone, it can't be good.

"What the hell are you saying? It can be to your advantage!"

It's a little closer now. I can only hope he's not going to take out his frustration on me.

No. He will have to open that cuff at some point. That will be my moment.

Whatever it is he drugged me with is still heavy in my system. Despite my frantic state, I can barely keep my eyes open. How long has it been? Did Sienna realize that something was wrong, or did she simply think I bailed?

She must have spoken with Will. They might alert the authorities. Something has to happen.

⁓∙ℓℓ⁓

"It can be to your advantage!"

What the hell is wrong with these men he's known for a decade? Kevin Hollis was certain he knew them inside out. Family, loyalty, legacy, pitting one against the other. Organized crime thrives on those concepts, and he should know, because he's benefited from that fact quite a bit.

Yet, they are not acting as he had expected, and everything is spiraling out of control.

Francesco Caruso flat out laughed at him at the idea that he might want to use Courtney in his war against the Flynns.

"You are ridiculous, Sergeant Hollis. I want that stubborn old man to admit that my nephew didn't kill Tommy. I have no interest in his daughter-in-law, and from what I hear, neither does he. Actually, word on the street is that you might be protecting the real killer."

Don't say it.

Don't go there.

"Some might even say it's you. I tell you what, Hollis, stay away from us. Tommy Flynn might not have been a friend, but we tolerated him well enough, and whoever killed him, caused us one hell of a headache. Let's hope for your sake I'm not going to find out it was you."

His tone turned cold on the last words.

Hollis knew when he was being threatened, and he knew if Caruso made good on that threat, there was nowhere to go for him. Certainly not to Rory Flynn who would send his own goons the moment he learned the truth.

He didn't respond but simply ended the call, feeling sick to his stomach. It was time to engage the emergency protocol. Damn Courtney Flynn and her curiosity, damn her for getting in bed with Sienna Caruso who had more resources at her disposal than the average police station.

He had his reasons. There might even be people he could have explained them to, except if their names were Caruso or Flynn.

Fortunately, he had never harbored many illusions about their loyalty toward him. It would just have to get a bit messier than expected.

Hollis' next call went to his wife. "It's time," he said.

Chapter Twenty-Six

S ienna Caruso was far from what Rory had made her out to
be, not that it came as a surprise. Saoirse had met her briefly
before, but never talked to her much. Here, in close quarters
with the woman, she could feel her despair, uncomfortably re-
latable.

Saoirse had never forgotten a moment of the night Tommy
Flynn was killed. She should have been there, no matter what
Rory, Kevin Hollis, or even Tommy had said. She remembered
despair, and she was going to jump at a chance to hold Hollis
responsible for what he had done.

Two birds, one stone. Everyone had waited long enough.

"Okay," she said after ending the call. "He isn't at work, called
in sick a couple of days ago. Let's go check on him."

Sienna

S aoirse is driving above the speed limit, which I appreciate, and yet I have to stop myself from tapping my fingers on the dashboard. I have faith in our abilities, and the firearms we carry, and yet this could go wrong in so many ways.

History. Present. One figure at the center of it, and he is much more dangerous than we imagined. Either way, we must stop him now. Bring Courtney and Oliver home, and then even Rory will have to admit he's been wrong all this time, not that he's a priority at the moment.

We drive up to Hollis' home which, to no one's surprise, is a whole lot more luxurious than someone on his salary could afford. The Hollises have not been subtle about spending the money that Kevin's corruption on the job brought them.

Saoirse has barely stopped the car when I open the door, all but jump out and head over to the entrance. A woman in her late forties with meticulous hair and make-up is hefting a large suitcase into the trunk of an SUV. According to my file, it's Hollis' wife Pam.

"Mrs. Hollis? My name is Sienna Caruso. Is your husband here?"

"No, he's not," she dismisses me. "I'm sorry, I don't have time."

"Well, you'll have to make time. How come he's not here if he called in sick at work?"

Pam regards me with a calculating gaze. "You're not the police, are you? I don't have to answer to you."

"How about I take a look myself then?"

"No!" she cries when I march towards the front door. I spin around when I hear a pained yelp, just in time to see Saoirse wrestle the gun from Pam's hand.

"You can thank me later," she tells me. "All right, Mrs. Hollis, now cut the bullshit."

I can't help but being impressed. So is Pam, apparently.

"You have no right! You have to let me go, or I'll call the police!"

"And tell them what, that you pulled a gun on us when we were asking for Kevin's whereabouts? I'll take my chances," Saoirse says.

I'm not quite sure if Pam's distress is real, but she seems to deflate in front of us, starting to cry.

"I need to get my kids. Let me go."

"Tell us where Kevin is, and we will."

"I don't know! He was going to call me back. He hasn't yet. But I need to pick up the kids from school."

Saoirse sends me a quizzical look, and I nod. It sounds true.

"Ms. Hollis, do you have other properties?"

"Why do you want to know that?" Pam turns to Saoirse, "Why don't you ask your boss Flynn? I'm sure he knows."

"We're asking *you*." I silently congratulate her on her calm tone when all I want is to shake Pam Hollis.

Even with tears glistening in her eyes, Pam stares back at me in defiance.

"Kevin has done nothing wrong. Are you going to hurt him?"

"Hurt him?" Saoirse asks in disbelief. "Look, we have reason to believe that he has abducted Courtney Flynn and her son. If you don't tell us, we could just go inside and go through your papers. I'm sure we'll find something, but then it might be too late for them. Do you really want their blood on your hands?"

"The cabin," Pam mumbles.

"What did you say? Where is it?" I asked. At this rate, I might still shake her.

"Okay, I'll tell you, but let me go get the kids."

The moment after she has related the address, Saoirse cuffs her to the wrought-iron gate.

"Hey! You promised!"

I don't waste any time waiting for the end of that dialogue. It's even better if Saoirse stays with her.

"Sienna! What the hell are you doing?"

Back in the car, I make a U-turn and drive past the two women, both angry at me, if for a different reason. I couldn't care less.

I'm going to find Hollis, find Courtney and Oliver, and end this mess for good. A not entirely unselfish part of me still harbors hope far beyond that goal, but I won't let it distract me either.

Traffic is a bit heavier than when we came here, and I spend a good amount of time cursing, honking, and hitting the steering wheel. For the majority of the past few years, I had been holing myself up in her office, making clever moves, commanding meetings, growing the family business to what I had hoped would be the pride of Francesco and Simona. At times, I've been fairly proud of myself, but now it feels like glossing over what else was going on, could cost me.

Why didn't I call them out earlier? The war games with the Flynns cost both families, and innocent bystanders. We can't go on like this. I'll make that clear once I have dealt with the immediate situation.

When traffic stops altogether for a moment, I call Courtney again, still only getting the voicemail.

"You'll be okay," I say out loud. "And no one's ever going to take Oliver away from you. I promise."

In the car next to me, two teens are pointing and laughing, and I send them a glare and an unmistakable gesture involving my middle finger. It makes me feel only slightly better.

At least, the vehicle in front of me starts moving, and the moment I can, I take the next exit. About fifteen, twenty more minutes to go until I'll reach Hollis' property—and the point of no return.

Chapter Twenty-Seven

Courtney

I overhear enough of the conversation to know Hollis is in trouble, and by uncomfortable proxy, so am I. I don't even have time to be mad at what he's apparently trying—or the fact that none of the big players care enough about me to even negotiate for my release.

The man whose son I was married to.

The man whose niece I'm dating.

When Hollis returns, there's a frantic look on his face. He tries to call someone else, another time, cursing when it goes to voicemail both times.

"You said you were going to let me see Oliver. Where is he?"

He actually laughs in my face.

"You were so easy. I knew you would be, I've seen how you spoil him. He would have grown up soft, just like Tommy was. I have no fucking idea where Oliver is now."

"What?"

I can't be certain. This man has lied so many times he probably doesn't even know what the truth is anymore, and I doubt that he cares.

"I don't have time for this." He produces the key to the cuffs, and with a conceited grin, waves his forefinger in front of me. "We're going on a little ride. Don't try anything. I know Tommy never got you to learn how to shoot a gun, so whatever you think you can do, it won't work."

"Where are we going?"

My mind is reeling with the possibilities. If he has Oliver and Alice, where are they? Will anyone find them in time?

And if he doesn't...Did Rory make good on his threats? He believed in the stories about the Carusos because they gave him a reason for revenge. He's not going to change his mind. Am I being unfair, I'm not sure, but it's hard to be considerate with a gun to my head.

"None of your concerns. Get up."

Hollis has it wrong. The gun is a concern, a big one, but a couple of steps towards the water, and my mind goes into alarm mode.

"Get on the damn boat!" He doesn't have any patience left, but I can barely move. The gun is in my back now, and for a few second, the fear of everything, Oliver's fate, a madman threatening me with a loaded weapon, and the dark waters in front of me, rob me of my breath.

I take a shaky step, and almost fall, but make it safely to the other side, and onto the boat, my knees jelly. I hold myself up against the wall of the cabin, as far away from the railing as possible. Between the gun and the water, was there ever a chance to run? I'll never know, but I'll have to do something.

This can't be the end. I have so many more things to do in my life, spend it with the people I love. Kevin Hollis can't change that.

Chapter Twenty-Eight

Sienna

I can still hear the sound of the engine when I arrive at the boathouse, see the boat in the distance. Too late. I'm not willing to accept that. I might be desperate, but I have skills, and little left to lose. There are similar properties around, and I don't care if I have to rent or steal to get to Courtney.

The old me, sitting in that office, might have been shocked, but I've spent too much time out in the real world lately, getting a different perspective on family, loyalty, the truth.

All I know is that I can't wait. I can see another dock from here, with a lonely boat swaying in the water. There's no road, but I jog along the shore in little time, grateful that I've been keeping in shape.

The thoughts are chasing one another in my mind.

Does Hollis know about Courtney's apparent fear of water? Does he plan to use it against her? I don't plan on waiting to find out.

When I reach the dinghy, I wonder if I have to make use of some abilities Courtney might call shady but would come in handy now. Nico taught me those skills back then when it was all fun and games. Cars, boats, I know how to rig them if necessary. It turns out that I don't have to go that far. I pull the cord to get the motor going, thinking that I'll pay the owner for the gas, or if something should happen to this boat.

Not a problem.

But first, I have to reach them. Hollis has quite a head start. I can see the outline of him, but not Courtney.

What if...

No. Now is not the time for worst-case scenarios, not when I'm this close.

I can tell when he's spotted me because he fires the first shot right away. I duck, then return fire. One of his next shots hits the side of the boat, and I say a silent apology. I might have to buy the owners a new one, but so be it. I stay down while I steer closer, trying to catch a glimpse of Courtney.

Then I see her. He's hiding behind her like the coward he is, pointing his gun at her temple.

"Get lost, Sienna! Go away, or I swear I'll kill her!"

I keep my weapon trained on him.

"I'll be faster. Do you want to take the risk? You can still come out of this alive!"

He laughs bitterly. "Between your uncle and her father-in-law, I'm already dead. Do you hear me? I don't care. About you, or her. I'll gain a little time for Pam and our kids to get away, and that will be the end, Sienna. For all of us."

"But that's the thing, Kevin. Pam isn't going anywhere."

Even with the fair distance, I can see his eyes narrowing.

"What did you do?"

I don't answer, just seek Courtney's gaze and hold it for a second or so. She's frightened. This has to end.

I plan to shoot the asshole's leg, but before I do, she tears herself away and jumps over the railing.

Kevin Hollis sputters an expletive, and then another one when I make the shot. There's another boat driving towards us from the other side. The Coast Guard. I will likely need a lawyer today, but I'll deal with that once Courtney is safe, which she isn't at the moment.

When I see Hollis drop his weapon as instructed by the Coast Guard over the megaphone, I do the same, but I don't wait for them to board the boat.

I jump into the water and swim straight to where Courtney is struggling to stay afloat. She's going under, resurfacing again, spitting water.

Finally, I reach her and hold on to her, though I know we're not safe yet. She's panicking as I knew she would, nearly pulling both of us under.

"You'll be okay! I got you!"

I know, in this kind of situation, knowing and feeling are two different things, but after what seems like an eternity, she relaxes against me.

"Let's get you out of the water."

"I agree," someone says dryly, and when I look up, the woman is standing in the boat I abandoned, reaching out a hand.

She gets first Courtney, then me to safety.

"You're here," Courtney whispers.

"Of course. I'm sorry it took me so long." She rests in my embrace for a moment before she turns to the newcomer. "I love you, but I kind of meant her...Agent Farmer. Ryan."

I'm dumbfounded for a couple of obvious reasons. One is easily explained: The agent was probably on the case during the investigation into Tommy Flynn's murder, given his profile. That still doesn't explain why she's here now, but I'm sure I'll find out.

The other...*love*. It warms me up inside, even as my body has other ideas, my teeth starting to chatter. It's not that cold today, but a lot has happened in little time, stress taking its toll.

"I got a call from a reliable source," Agent Farmer reveals everything and nothing. "Let's get you two dry, and then we'll have a conversation about everything that happened."

"Ryan, please, remember she fished me out of the water."

Agent Farmer, Ryan, pats Courtney's shoulder. "I won't forget it. Come on. There are people waiting for you."

"Did you find Oliver and Alice?" Courtney asks, sounding very young. My heart goes out to her.

"We did," Farmer says. "They're unharmed."

I can feel Courtney sag with relief. She pulls herself together, straightens, but she's still struggling to find the words.

"I don't think Agent Farmer minds if we go to see them first?" I test the waters, so to speak.

"Where?" The single word is a plea. Courtney is clearly at the end of her rope. She's entitled, though I'm certain that seeing Oliver will make all the difference in the world. I realize I need that too.

"We'll take you to them," Farmer explains.

I swear, the woman was this close to rolling her eyes at me, but maybe, she, too, can't resist the lure of happy endings. Mother and son reunited. No one died, this time.

And I think I'll have to call my lawyer too.

But first I pull Courtney close to me.

Chapter Twenty-Nine

Courtney

I am alive, and on my way to see Oliver. He and Alice are unharmed, and I...mostly am. Sienna came to find me, and I don't need anything else to call it a successful day.

I can't bring myself to think about all the implications, how Hollis shot and killed Tommy, and covered it up for years, Rory seizing the moment to take Oliver back to the mansion, or the fact that Sienna will have to answer for her actions as well.

Given that she stole a boat to rescue me, and it was Hollis who put some bullets in it, I hope the authorities will be lenient with her. She deserves it.

More than Rory who will soon get a visit from an angry mother, his fiercest competitor, and the FBI.

The mansion has stellar security, but even they can't do much when the FBI arrives with a warrant. As soon as we are inside, I ignore all of Ryan's warnings and run upstairs to the suite Oliver and I occupied after Tommy's death. I did that, insisted that the two of us didn't need quarters like before. No one cared. No one in this house ever did.

I yank the door open and stop cold at the sight of Rory sitting on the floor with Oliver, the two of them playing with colorful blocks. Alice sits on a chair in the corner, her expression impassive until she realizes that I'm not alone. The relief showing on her face is instant.

"Mommy!" Oliver yells, and all but flies into my arms. "Look what Grandpa gave me."

I hold him close for as long as I need to in order to breathe properly again, tears clouding my vision. "That's very nice of Grandpa," I whisper. "Did you say thank you?"

"Yes."

That's good because it will be a while before the next opportunity. I straighten, not letting go of his hand when I finally face Rory, who has the gall to be irritated with the interruption.

"Courtney, I didn't invite you here."

"That's fine. I have no intention of staying. And I'm taking Oliver with me. What were you thinking?"

"I'm thinking..." He raises himself up to his full height. "He's my grandson. I can see him whenever I please, and you have no right to keep him from me."

Does he really think that after today, he can intimidate me? It's almost laughable. I heard part of the phone calls. I know Hollis was in touch with him.

"Just like you had no right to send the corrupt cop on your payroll after me? Tell me, what was the plan?"

He makes a dismissive gesture. "I didn't send anyone after you. You've always been paranoid. I don't know anything about—"

"We'll see about that," Ryan has come inside the room after me, her colleagues following her. Oliver regards them curiously, and I'm grateful he's distracted. Now that the danger is past, I'm so mad again I can barely breathe. How dare he?

"You might remember me, Special Agent Farmer with the FBI. Mr. Flynn, I have to ask you to come with us."

"You can't do that," he says with an incredulous laugh.

"Oh, I can. I have the paperwork. And I thought you'd prefer to do this quietly, given your grandson is still in the room."

He shoots me another furious look, to which I almost laugh. I wasn't the one who called Ryan, but I don't care to correct the possible misconception, just hold his gaze.

"Can we come back soon, Grandpa?" Oliver asks, his hopeful tone heartbreaking. But there are some uncomfortable truths we can't evade.

"Of course," Rory says, ruffling his hair before he joins Ryan out of the room, his head held up high.

I fall to my knees to hug Oliver again.

"I'm so happy to be here for this. If I'm honest? All of it."

I look up to see Sienna standing in the doorway and hold out my hand. She joins us, and for a moment, all complications that still lie ahead, are far away.

It doesn't matter how we started out, or how unlikely a future might be—this feels like, this is family.

And love.

Catching up with Ryan Farmer, one of the agents who came to the mansion after Tommy was killed, comes with mixed emotions. I'm glad that her source had the presence of mind to alert her. I have an idea as to who that might be.

I am still so grateful that Sienna came for me, and I hope she won't be in trouble over the methods she employed.

Most of all I'm still very much shaken, but happy to have Oliver with me.

Of all of us, he had the least terrifying day. If I can give Rory credit for anything, it's that he made what's basically my son's abduction, look like a fun outing with Grandpa.

Oliver never learned what Alice, Sienna, and I had to go through.

That's where my goodwill ends when Ryan shows me what else he's been up to in the past twenty-four hours.

"This is a bit unorthodox," she reminds me when we sit in an office at the police station she occupies for the moment. "I thought you deserved to know."

"He took my son while one of his, I don't know what to call Hollis? A foot soldier? Took me and threatened to kill me. How much worse can it get?"

Ryan doesn't smile at the joke, though she looks sympathetic. "Hollis has an entire archive of recorded conversations. Including the one with Flynn today."

I don't expect anything good, and yet my jaw drops when I hear the dialogue between the two men. I feel the chill returning when I remember parts of it, something Hollis said.

And then Rory: *"Are you really that stupid? I don't give a damn about her. She made her bed when she left us. I want my grandson. You let me know when it's done."*

"That's...a bit harsh. Not a surprise, but still harsh."

I take a big hasty sip of my coffee, wincing when it burns my tongue. I have a hard time warming up, and it's not all physical. I look over to where Oliver is playing in a corner. He's safe. He's happy. Nothing else matters. And yet...

"I agree. Of course, it's more than a moral question. Hollis gave us a bit of a treasure trove."

"That means he gets a deal?"

She gives me a wry smile. "We're not there yet. It's not like he came to us willingly. I'm just saying it will be interesting to go through all of it."

"Can I ask you something?"

"Sure, go ahead."

"Do you believe now that I never had anything to do with...the business, whatever it is? I was just trying to keep my head above water."

She acknowledges that with a nod.

"That outcome never sat well with us, and now we have proof against Hollis. I wish it hadn't taken that long."

"What about Sienna? She was only trying to save me."

"Yeah." She looks thoughtful for a moment. "Stealing property that then got damaged, she will have to answer for that. We'll take the circumstances into consideration."

"Please do. You won't find her in Hollis' archive. Her uncle, maybe. Hollis called him earlier."

"Yes, we know. Ms. Flynn, I'm glad you're all right. I hope you can move past this."

"A really hot bath, a few glasses of wine, and an indulgent meal will help," I say, finally eliciting a smile from the stoic woman. I always found her hard to read, but I realize she was never the enemy. Neither was Sienna.

I hope that maybe she's going to be in the scenario I laid out for making me feel better, not that I need to mention that to the agent.

"I'm sure it won't hurt."

She gets to her feet, so I do the same.

"You can go home now. We might be in touch."

"Now that I know you're not looking to arrest me, the thought is a little less terrifying."

We shake hands, and Oliver and I can leave. Outside the room, I call Sienna, but the call goes to voicemail.

"Thank you again," I say. "We'll be at the inn. I hope you come by...later."

I wish there hadn't been that moment of hesitation, but I'll stop worrying when there's no more reason to.

Chapter Thirty

Sienna

I have asked my lawyer to join the conversation with the agent. Trust but verify. I am sure they will have their hands full with Kevin Hollis and Rory Flynn. Just in case...

"You don't like me very much, do you?"

Ryan Farmer looks up from her file with a frown.

I haven't met her before, but I've heard about her from Kendall, as she's one of her wife's former colleagues. By the book. Serious. Demons of her own.

Tia, my attorney, shoots me a quizzical look, and I shrug. It's been a long day. I want to check on Courtney and Oliver. Hopefully be out of here in time for a leisurely dinner.

"Ms. Caruso, it's not about me. You understand—"

"I had to shoot at the man who was about to kill my girl-friend?"

"Sienna!" Tia warns me. "Agent Farmer, what my client is trying to say that her only incentive was to save Ms. Flynn's life in particular. The owner of the boat will be fully reimbursed."

"That's to be expected. We contacted them, and they would like to speak to you." Farmer's expression shows that she can hardly believe what she's about to say. "A little heads-up, they think of this as an adventure, a story to tell their grandchildren. Which means they'll be fine as long as you pay for the damage, including any increased insurance coverage."

"Yeah, sure. That's not a problem."

No, she doesn't like me, I can tell. *Her* problem.

"Good to hear. We might have some additional questions regarding a phone call Mr. Hollis made today to your Uncle Francesco."

"Fine. Ask away. I didn't know anything about that, as you can imagine."

"Agent Farmer, may I remind you that we're here solely to clear up the incident involving my client rescuing Ms. Flynn?" Tia intervenes.

I appreciate that she never gets nervous, even though she's probably a bit irritated with me now. I can live with that.

"Given that the call took place today, and its content, it's interesting you don't know anything about it," Agent Farmer addresses me, ignoring Tia.

"Well, it might be interesting to you, but it's the truth. Let's be honest, shall we? You are aware that my family, and Courtney's, have history. I'm glad we were able to clear up some things today, like the fact that my cousin didn't shoot Tommy Flynn. I hope you're not suggesting I staged my attempt at getting to Courtney before Hollis could kill her. I didn't know about whatever deal Hollis was trying to make, and I'm pretty sure Francesco didn't want anything to do with it either. But that, you'll have to ask him."

"Don't worry, we will."

I have no illusions about any additional questions she might have. I've been audited before. My books are clean. I hope the same is true for Francesco and Simona, though I'm afraid I already know the answer—and what they'll think of me drawing the FBI's attention to the family. They can't disown me, I have too much of my own money invested in the company.

A part of me, the younger Sienna who depended on the two of them, feels sick at the thought.

Another, grown-up me, is just as sick understanding that they knew Hollis had Courtney, and they chose, what, not to get involved? Something's got to give.

"Will that be all for now?" I ask, and Farmer gives me a curt nod.

"There are still some loose ends to tie up. I'd appreciate it if you didn't leave town."

"Where would I go?" I ask, and she acknowledges that this is a rhetorical question. I have some family matters to address, some maybe more pleasant than others. Some more difficult.

In the hallway, Tia is all business.

"We should go to my office now and discuss strategy. It's only a matter of time until they come knocking with those additional questions, and we want to be prepared—"

"Tomorrow," I cut her off.

"But Sienna..."

"I'll authorize a payment for the boat, then I want to go home. The rest, any potential charges, I trust you to come up with some ideas, and we'll talk tomorrow."

She doesn't look happy.

"As you wish."

"It will be fine. I can't deny today was something, but we'll figure it out. Well...You will figure it out. I have faith in you."

Her features soften with the smile, making me wonder how much of today's over the top emotions are visible on my face.

I stole a boat. I got shot at. But it's all worth it because Courtney is alive and well.

Now, I need to convince myself.

Chapter Thirty-One

Courtney

I keep checking my phone, but there is no response from Sienna yet. Should I go back to the Grand Palace, her suite? I don't even know where she lives. I am exhausted, but there are a few things that can't wait until tomorrow. I need to speak to her.

I also need to apologize to Will and Alice, and so the hot bath will have to wait.

Back at our temporary home, I get Oliver ready for bed. They gave him a sandwich and some candy at the station—I couldn't get anything down, but he's crashing now. When Oliver is asleep, I hurry straight to Will's office and knock.

"Can I talk to you for a moment?" I ask when he calls me in.

Will is sitting behind his desk, looking pensive. Before he has a chance to answer, I blurt out, "I am so sorry. I never meant for anything to happen to Alice—"

"Court, wait, I know—"

"And I can understand if you want to fire me on the spot. I had no idea—" Maybe that's not right. Maybe I should have known that Rory would use the first opportunity.

"Courtney Flynn!"

His tone is a little sharper now, and I shut up.

"I don't intend to fire you," he says. "I know it wasn't your fault. I am just...wow. This was quite the day."

"Yes it was." There's no denying that.

"Are you okay?"

That's a loaded question.

"I think so," is as truthful as I can get. "I'll be better once we know all the facts. As much as the police will share with us, that is."

"I never imagined...Is Sienna here?"

"No. I haven't reached her yet. Since..." I don't have to elaborate.

"Look, you do what you need to do. I can assure you that I don't blame you for what happened, and neither does Alice. How about we start there?"

"Thank you," I say, my throat going tight. He gets up to walk around the desk and gives me a brief hug, comforting. At this moment, I know what I need. And it can't wait any longer.

I go up to my room to make sure Oliver is still sleeping soundly. It's hard for me to be still, but I sit down for a few minutes, simply watch him breathe. I almost lost him.

I can forgive a lot of things people do out of love. The same things, done out of greed for power, it's different. At the same time, I'm still astonished and a little proud. Maybe delusional, but I did literally jump ship when I needed to, despite a fear of drowning. That's quite the metaphor, though the experience was harrowingly real.

A knock on the door jolts me out of my thoughts, my immediate concern for another crisis turning into profound gratitude when I see Sienna on the other side of it. I don't know how she does it at the end of a day like this, but the only sign of today's ordeal is that she looks a little tired. The rest is just her usual perfection.

I have so many things to tell her, but before I do, I pull her inside and wrap my arms around her.

"Are you going to be okay? They're not coming after you, are they?"

Okay, I'm just not that perfect. My voice is brittle.

"Not yet," she says, a hint of amusement to her tone. "You want to run away with me in case they do?"

I lean into her warmth.

"I don't know, I'm kind of tired of running. I'm pretty tired, period."

"I can relate to that," she says with a sigh. "I can go if you want..."

"No. No, please stay."

She steps back, giving me that enigmatic smile that got me hooked from the start.

"In that case, do you think we can get any decent take-out around here?"

"I think we could give it a try."

Sienna kisses me, softly at first, then with the promise of so much more. Perhaps words can wait, though I don't think food can.

"More of this," I promise. "But how about we check the take-out options first?"

Sienna laughs. "Your priorities are mine. I'm starving."

Sometime in the near future, words will be necessary. For now, the fact that she's here and obviously ready to stay fills me with hope.

It doesn't feel treacherous any longer.

It's real this time.

Finally, we have food on the coffee table in the sitting area, having dinner together while it's dark outside, and Oliver is firmly immersed in dreamland without the nightmares that might haunt us for a while.

But for the first time since the police brought the horrific news, I feel like I can breathe, take my life into my own hands again.

I know that Sienna has her own regrets and worries to wrestle with when it comes to the future of her family, but she's here, with us, a little out of place even in casual clothes. That means everything.

"Are you going to eat, or just look at me?" she asks, her tone mildly teasing.

On this day of all days, I can't get flustered. I laugh.

"I don't know but you are extremely appealing to me."

"I'm very flattered. But eat. It's getting cold."

I heed her advice, though moments later I feel the need to say what's on my mind.

"I think I need to go back to the city. Not because of what happened here, Will said he doesn't blame me...It's the right decision."

"You're reconsidering my job offer?"

"Actually, no." Her face falls ever so slightly, nothing someone who hasn't observed her closely would notice. "Please, don't take this the wrong way. I can't take a job where I'll be sleeping with the boss. It wouldn't be right."

"So, you have it all planned out?"

"I wish," I admit. "All I know is that I need to find my footing, do what's right for Oliver and me, and I think it's the best place to do it. Move forward with my life. And I really hope that you're going to be in it."

It's not flattery that puts the smile on her face this time. I sense relief and gratitude, and I get to my feet. She does the same.

"So, you're saying yes? Even though there's going to be a mild amount of chaos which seems to follow me wherever I go?"

"Mild," she repeats, amused. "Darling, I know a bit about chaos. It doesn't frighten me. I'm in."

Her calling me darling sends a pleasant shiver down my spine, but even if Oliver wasn't right here in the room with us, I don't think I could do anything, with my body finally relaxing, and the wine we're having with dinner kicking in.

There's no missing the relevance and emphasis of her statement though.

"Thank you for rescuing me. I have many ideas about how to pay you back. It might take years."

Her answer is a warm, tight embrace. I needed that too. But most of all I'm eager to learn all the facets of this extraordinary woman I was supposed to consider the enemy.

Chapter Thirty-Two

Sienna

Spending a quiet evening with Courtney, holding her close all night, having breakfast together this morning, it's the quiet before the storm.

We both know it, and so while Oliver is chatting animatedly with one of the servers, Courtney asks me again, "Are you really going to be okay?"

Last night was all indulgence and sweet. Today, we take everything we've learned and gained, back to the real world. What we've come to mean to each other. Something that already looks and feels like love, like family.

A family where people stand up for each other, not expect blind loyalty.

I'm on my second coffee when an irate Francesco calls, and I get up and leave the room, let him rage on. In the wake of his tirade, there's a heavy silence.

"Are you done?" I ask.

"How could you do that to us, Sienna? You have betrayed the family!"

Those words are near meaningless now, and I have to catch my breath. I am grieving everything I thought we were, finally understanding it was never true.

"How, Uncle Francesco? I didn't do anything. I had never even met Kevin Hollis before yesterday. That's not true for you, and you knew he was bad news."

"I didn't invite him to dinners like Rory Flynn did," he returns. "He was useful for a while."

"Yeah, I can see that now. I can also see how you could have been a bit more useful when he offered up Courtney to you, as what? Bait? You could have come to me, or better yet, alerted the authorities, because when they shoot at criminals, they have a lot less explaining to do!"

"You are delusional. Why would I get in the middle of it, when Flynn—"

"I don't give a fuck about Flynn!"

The woman who walks by with her teenage daughter gives me a startled look, her jaw dropping slightly. The teen gives me a thumbs up. I wait until they're out of earshot to continue this unfortunate exchange.

"Look, I didn't sic the FBI on you. You withholding information about Courtney's abduction did that, and you'll have to deal with it. And you have the audacity to accuse me of betraying the family? Everything I've done since I could walk was for the good of the family, and everyone's paycheck tells the story. Don't you think it's a good thing that Nico can finally come home?"

I am irritated and disgusted. Sure, Flynn seems to truly love his grandson, but beyond that love, grief for Tommy and family connections, he's been enjoying the ongoing battle far too much. I am still coming to terms with the fact that these two men, one of whom I've considered a father figure, someone to look up to, for a long time, are basically the same.

It's not about family. It's about winning at all costs, no matter who gets hurt.

It's not the life or the future I want, for me, or the people I love.

"It is," he finally acknowledges.

"I'm glad we can agree on something."

"You had no right—"

"This conversation is over, Uncle Francesco. I have other matters to tend to."

"They're going to come after you too," he threatens. "If you don't have our backs, why would we have yours?"

I end the call and go back to join Courtney and Oliver.

I have no doubt that he'll try to make my life harder, and I'll deal with it. I never understood it as much as I do now: Yes, they gave me a home, food, clothing, an education, and I'll be forever grateful.

But since I've become the CEO and face of Grand Palace hotels and resorts, I've been utterly alone. I had no help while the rest of my family engaged in more or less legal pursuits, expecting me to maintain a clean front.

Well, it's not just a front to me. It is the real thing, and I'm proud of it. I don't even blame Courtney for not wanting a job with me, because her reasoning is sound.

Across the room, our eyes meet, and I can't help smiling, even knowing the challenges ahead.

I can't be her boss because I plan on sleeping with her in the future. For many years to come.

"Sienna, come back!" Oliver urges. "I want to show you something."

Who am I to argue?

Some connections in life are more important than others, and I'm certain I've found mine.

———⁓⁓⁓———

The FBI didn't have enough to arrest Francesco, and while we are not on the best terms, he had to grudgingly admit that the chain of events helped bring Nico home—and his wife whom he met during his half forced, half chosen exile.

Work has been gruelling, for me, for Courtney who started a new job with another hotel in the city.

Tonight, it's finally time for something fun, as the Grand Palace is hosting a vernissage by Sela Andras.

I've extended invitations to everyone, though I already know that I won't see Uncle Francesco or Aunt Simona tonight.

Nico and his wife Caterina are here, and so is the artist, Alessandra Falcone, with her wife Mia. Not everyone knows about her alter ego creating gorgeous nudes. Like me, Alessandra sits at the top of a corporation, and that position always requires keeping secrets. Given the time of day and the adult nature of the works, Nico's daughter and Oliver are with a babysitter right now. Alice, who was spooked but not deterred by her experience, has agreed to watch them.

I spot Kendall Mancini and her wife Robyn having champagne as they study the life-sized paintings, though the looks they give each other are even more appreciative. It makes me smile. Word is that they never got out of the honeymoon phase, and it's obvious.

It makes my mind wander, too, into what's nothing more than a dream at this moment. For a long time, I thought it was entirely out of reach for me, but that's no longer true.

The future is wide open.

I go to check on my own significant other, but when I reach the lobby, Courtney is coming down the stairs, in a blue gown she didn't let me see before the event. Well, that's good practice for another event that could be in our near future.

My breath catches in my throat as I watch her, the unspoken question in her expression. Yes, I will tell her over and over again. Anyone who thought she wasn't enough, not representing or deserving the family enough, was wrong.

We know better.

I wait until she's reached the bottom of the stairs, and, given the fact that there's no time for heavy subjects at this moment, I reach for her hand.

"You look amazing," I say. "I can't decide whether I want you in this dress or out of it."

Her words belie the somewhat shy smile.

"I think given some time, we can do both."

"I like that idea. Soon. Are you ready?"

"I so am. I've heard great things about the artist."

I can't help smiling so hard it nearly hurts. She's heard them from me, of course. Together, we walk back into the room, and having her by my side is more natural than anything I've ever felt. One day, she'll know all my secrets, and the thought doesn't even scare me any longer.

"I love you," I whisper, and Courtney turns to me. No one has ever looked at me with that much warmth and devotion, and it melts the last bit of ice around my heart I thought I needed to protect myself.

"I love you too."

It's all I need to hear. The future starts right now.

Epilogue

Saoirse

"If anything happens to me, make sure Courtney is safe."

"Nothing's going to happen to you," she had told Tommy, feigning indignation. *"You don't think I know how to do my job?"*

Those words came back to haunt her, but Saoirse had been determined to make good on one promise. She had nurtured her connections, making sure a certain Special Agent would be there at the right time. No one was completely innocent, and people like Farmer understood that.

Even before Hollis took an interest in Courtney, Saoirse had known that someday, she'd need to position herself for a smooth exit. When he escalated, Agent Farmer had come through.

Now that the job was done, she could start over for real, and no one would try to stop her.

Rory was busy fending off legal troubles, and he knew she wouldn't betray him or his family. Courtney didn't need Saoirse any longer—she had found love and a family with Sienna Caruso. There was no reason why she should feel wistful about it. It was her choice to cut ties with anyone called Flynn.

As a last favor, she would keep Tommy's secrets. He was a hero once more to his family. The Carusos no longer considered him the enemy, and a truce between the families was established again.

What they didn't know was that he'd been talking about getting out, had made plans even. Move Courtney and Oliver to a cottage in the Irish countryside, live happily ever after. Those plans were as idyllic as they were unreal, but that hadn't stopped him. They had talked about his options, including turning state's evidence. He had all the information to make powerful men go down.

Now, thanks to Tommy, Saoirse had that information. She didn't intend to do anything with it, except in the case she should need it as a bargaining chip—or life insurance.

She left a single rose at the foot of the marble angel and walked back to where she had parked her motorcycle. Time to get out of town, towards a new day.

About the Author

B arbara Winkes writes sapphic crime drama and Christ- mas romance. She loves writing characters who get the job done, whether it's stopping a predator or saving cherished traditions—while still making time for love. She lives with her wife in Quebec City.

barbarawinkes.com

Acknowledgments

T hank you –

    As always, Dominique, for believing in me (and the beautiful cover art), my fellow authors for the conversations and support, and my readers. You're simply the best!

Also by Barbara Winkes

The Crossing Lines Trilogy
Undercover
Redemption
Vengeance

The Connected Series
Promised to the Queen
Drawn to the Enemy
Tempted by the Protector